THE ANNALS OF A QUIET VALLEY

By

A Country Parson

Edited by John Watson, F.L.S.

Author of "Sylvan Folk"

"Nature and Woodcraft"

&c. &c.

British Library Cataloguing-in-Publication Data
A catalogue record for this book is available from the
British Library

The Head of the Valley

To

J. & M. T.

TWO WORTHY YEOMEN

MY FIRST AND LIFE-LONG FRIENDS

IN THE DALE

LIST OF ILLUSTRATIONS.

PREFATORY NOTE.

THE contents of the following pages mainly concern a single valley in the English Lake District—a dale which need not, perhaps, be further particularised than is done in the text. The valley of the book is, however, a compound of several originals which form one general watershed, and, geographically, are not widely separated.

Perhaps these pages may reflect the lives and doings of one of the most interesting classes in the North—the race of yeoman, or 'statesman, a remnant only of which remains. *The History of the Northern Yeoman* has yet to be written, and these "Annals" have no pretension to set up any claim to stand in the place of that prospective work. My small contribution only plays round the fringe of the subject; it does not aspire to more than this. I know and have known one characteristic dale intimately, and having loved it, this is my tribute. The great mountains still hem it in, but the old fell-folk are gone; comparative strangers have taken their place. With every appreciation of these, I cannot think the change is for the better. It may not matter economically, but the old sentiment has utterly vanished — gone with those whose remains now fill the little churchyard. The church, too, has changed, and the parson—everything, in fact, but the illimitable mountains that shape the valley. So great has been the revolution, that a stranger driving up the mountain road would hardly recognise the dale as the one I have described. But there it is, and there it will remain. It is unknown to tourists, and they will be long in discovering it. Not that I am jealous of their intrusion—far otherwise — but the dale lies out of the beaten track. There is a way into it, but no way out—unless you know; and even then you must cross the wild moorlands to get back to civilisation.

But such as it is, or was—its people, its traditions, and its homesteads—I have tried to set it down. In conclusion, I must acknowledge my indebtedness to a local tract by "An Antiquary" for many of the more interesting facts especially concerning the home-life of the yeoman.

A COUNTRY PARSON.

THE

Annals of a Quiet Valley

CHAPTER I.

I WAS born in a primitive parsonage among the hills, and all our surroundings were as primitive as the old lichened house in which we were bred. My father was literally the "pore persoun" of the dale, as his father and grandfather had been before him. Although his stipend was small, he had a deep religious feeling anent the office to which he was called, and often expressed himself to the effect that his lot in life was precisely what he wished. "For drawen folk to heven by fairnesse and good example was his bisinesse." He held with Seneca, too, that those are the best instructors who teach in their lives and prove their words by their actions. In fact we had a motto worked in wool above the chimney-place to this effect, and upon the exemplification of it we often had little moral sermons. My mother was a notable woman in her way, and was come of a long line of "statesmen" or yeomen, but curiously enough (from my father's standpoint) she was a Quakeress. Her own kin had been followers of Fox since that memorable man preached from a haystack in the fold of one of their hill farms. I have heard it said that my mother was quite before her time in the matter of book learning, and I remember her to have held very broad and charitable views on whatever subjects interested her. As became her, she went with my father to church after their marriage, but there were two points on which they agreed to differ. These were "infant baptism" and the holding of the 37th Article. She had the strong opinions of her sect on the question of War, holding it incompatible with every precept of Christ. She urged that it was impossible to wage war on Christian principles, that Christian testimony against it was no cause of shame, and encouraged us to faithfulness in the matter. My father respected my mother's sentiments, but stoutly stuck to his " Article " nevertheless. This was the only cause of dissension in our family, but when the subject came up it was treated with becoming spirit on both sides. As I shall frequently have to speak of my mother, I will only repeat here that she was an admirable woman, and my father's opinion of her may be gathered from the following episode. Soon after my return from Oxford I received the appointment to the smallest church and the smallest living in England, and about that time I was on the lookout for a wife. I talked with my father on the subject, and he had but one advice to give. He referred me to the seventh line of the first page of his edition of Goldsmith's *Vicar of Wakefield* where I found marked the following words, " I chose my wife as she did her wedding-gown, not for a fine glossy surface, but for such qualities as would wear well." He continued that he had acted upon this advice, and had never had cause to regret it.

Among my first recollections was the being allowed to go to church for the first time—the church of which my father was clergyman.

This was a rude, barn-like building, and would have been difficult of identification as an ecclesiastical structure had it not been for the bell, the yew trees, and the few graves that surrounded it. Outside was a massive porch with seats, and (this I learned in after years) a "stoup" for holy water, a relic of pre-Reformation times. Inside, the church resembled a whitewashed barn, and the rafters were festooned with cobwebs. Smooth blue flags from the bed of the neighbouring stream covered the floor, and in winter a thick layer of straw was laid as a protection against damp and cold. The large square-backed pews were so deep that upon the visit of which I speak I was completely buried, and could see nothing of what was going on about me. What impressed me most was a pair of swallows that flew in and out of the open windows, and fed their callow young up somewhere among the dusty beams. My behaviour was so restless that I was not taken to church again for some time. Upon subsequent occasions my knowledge of church matters was widened. I was more favourably placed than at first, and in proportion as my range of vision was widened, so my interest increased. The pulpit from which my father preached was what is known as a "three-decker," and this was surmounted by a sounding board. Upon its quaintly carved oaken door was the date 1698. Within the Communion rails were a couple of spinning wheels, and heaped up by them several piles of carded wool. It was here that for eight hours each day my father kept school and taught, seated by his wheel the while. This, however, was only the case in summer, for in winter no school was held. The snow usually lay deeply in the valley, and travelling not only became difficult but dangerous. Keeping school in the way I have said was not begun by my father, it was so kept by my grandfather, and maybe before his time.

My grandfather I have only as yet casually mentioned. He was born in 1719, and being the youngest of twelve, and sickly, was, according to custom, bred a scholar. His "living" amounted to £43; but this he eked out in many ways—all of them honest, if not dignified. He tilled the glebe, laboured for the neighbouring farmers, spun and knitted the wool of his herdwicks, made wills, and conducted the limited correspondence of the whole parish. On the "lot" near to where we were bred was a small mere which contained grey trout and char, and I have heard it said that my grandfather taught the people to net the tarn, receiving by way of toll a half-penny for each draught of fishes. In addition to these offices, he added to his glebe a portion of ground which he rented, and did all the drudgery its working demanded. He also reclaimed a patch of mountain ground, kept a couple of cows, and had right of pasturage on the Common for a flock of fell sheep. At busy times, of washing the sheep in the fell becks, of shearing, and of haymaking, he went out to assist his neighbours, and in this way added to his income "in kind." Those of his parishioners who lived nearest gave a certain quantity of hay for each day of labour, while those further away contributed fleeces. The collection of these was left to the least busy part of the year; and in my grandfather's excursions among the hills he was always accompanied by an old white galloway, upon whose back the fleeces were carried crosswise in panniers. In all these matters in which he assisted, the old clergyman was more dexterous than his neighbours. My grandfather was possessed of great industry, but as I wish to be a veracious historian I must here set down one incident of his life which had a considerable bearing on it. After attaining the ministry of his native dale he married a wife with a fortune of £40, but neither appears to have demoralised him, for he remained in those habits of thrift and hard industry in which he had been long schooled.

I am sorry to have to say that this good man, unlike my father, refused absolutely to have dealings with the people called Quakers, because, as he expressed it, that stiff-necked generation "have some out-of-the-way and inconvenient notions anent the propriety of paying church dues." For the most part, however, he was charitably disposed, though in spite of this his economy was as wonderful as his industry. He supplied messes of broth to those who came to attend service from a distance on Sundays, and he sold them ale. In this matter he discriminated as follows:—That which was drunk in the vestry was charged at the rate of 4d. a quart, whilst the same swallowed on the road or in the churchyard was only 3d. This selling of ale may seem a strange inconsistency to the leading of a godly life, but the ale entailed much honest labour in the brewing, and the demand for it was, maybe, owing to some extent to the isolation of the mountain district. But all the quaintnesses of my grandfather came to an end in 1812, for in this year he died at the age of ninety-three, having lived among the same people for sixty-six years. He left behind him £2000, besides a large quantity of linen and woollen cloth, all of which was made during his teaching hours within the Communion rails of his little church.

Here is a picture of the old man written by one who visited him at his house during his lifetime, and I am told it is a faithful one. "I found him sitting at the head of a large square table, such as is commonly used in this country by the lower class of people, dressed in a coarse blue frock trimmed with black horn buttons, a checked shirt, a leathern strap about his neck for a stock, a coarse apron, and a pair of great wooden-soled shoes plated with iron to preserve them, with a child upon his knee, eating his breakfast. His wife and the remainder of his children were some of them engaged in waiting upon the others, the rest in teasing and spinning wool, at which trade he is a great proficient; and, moreover, when it is made ready for sale he will lay it by 16 lbs. or 32 lbs. weight on his back, and on foot, seven or eight miles, will carry it to market, even in the depth of winter. I was not much surprised at all this, as you may possibly be, having heard a great deal of it related before. But I must confess myself astonished with the alacrity and the good humour that appeared both in the clergyman and his wife, and more so at the sense and ingenuity of the clergyman himself."

After my grandfather's death many strange stories were told which the parishioners had not cared to relate whilst the old clergyman was living. As I verily believe, many good and excellent qualities were interred with his bones, but if the evil which he did lived after him, I am constrained to the opinion that it was hardly worthy to be called by that name. For instance, upon one occasion, he refused to obey the mandate of his Bishop, though I believe the refusal was due rather to his strong common-sense than to any want of respect for his spiritual superior. It came about in this wise. There had been a long period of drought, which had not only dried up the fell becks, but had burned the grass of the hill pastures to its roots. Rain was greatly needed, and unless it came soon the barn loads would be light. All nature drooped for want of water, and man and beast and land were parched alike. It was this state of things that moved the then Bishop of the diocese to request his clergy to offer up the prepared prayer of Mother Church "for rain." This my grandfather, after looking in what quarter the wind was, refused to do — or rather he simply omitted it. Some time subsequent to this the Bishop happened to be in our mountain parish, and mentioned the matter to the clergyman, though quite in a loving spirit. My grandfather replied that the Hard-Knott winds were not the rain-bringing ones, that it was no use offering up the prayer "for rain" so long as the winds blew from that quarter, and that he had no belief in flying in the face of Providence. The drought, he continued, was intended to teach us those lessons of dependence which we were far too apt to forget, and that the rain would come in its good season. And as the parishioners strongly upheld this view of the question, the matter was allowed to drop.

It was this same Bishop that years after used his influence to have my father appointed to a then vacant See in the north, the outcome of which was the following letter, addressed to him:—

"Regarding not so much your private interest as the interest of religion, I did what I could that the bishopric might be secured to you ; and the first character I gave of you to the king has, I doubt not, had some weight with his Majesty in his promoting of you to that See; which, not to mention the honour of it, will enable you to be of the utmost service to the Church of Christ. I am not ignorant how much rather you choose a private station; but if you consider the condition of the Church at this time, you cannot, I think, with a good conscience, refuse this burden, especially as it is a part of the Kingdom where no man is thought fitter than yourself to be of service to religion. Wherefore I charge you, before God, and as you will answer to Him, that, laying all excuses aside, you refuse not to assist your country and do what service you can to the Church of God. In the meantime, I can inform you that by the King's favour you will have the bishopric just in the condition in which Dr —— left it; nothing shall be taken from it, as hath been from some others. Wherefore, exhorting and beseeching you to be obedient to God's call herein, and not to neglect the duty of your function, I commend both you and this whole business to the Divine Providence," &c., &c.

Notwithstanding the pressing nature of this letter, it was without effect, for my father returned thanks, but declined the bishopric. Seeing that he considered his whole income in no other light than that of a fund to be managed for the common good, the emoluments attached to the offered See were no inducement to accept it. As he himself expressed it, he "was best acquainted with his own weakness, and knew himself unequal to the office."

Church life in the north at the time my grandfather held his "living" was of the most conservative description. At this early period the poor of the parish were entirely dependent upon their own township. And so it fell out that upon the application of a destitute family to one of the churchwardens a meeting was hastily called, and the family was "let out" to the highest bidder. As a rule there was great competition for the strong lads and lasses, and as these were "put up" the bidding grew quite animated. If hay or salving time happened to be at hand there was but little difficulty in disposing of the whole family.

Tithe was paid "in kind," and my grandfather was wont to stick a green branch upon each tenth sheaf of wheat, to mark that which was to be secured to the "tithe barn," which stood near his house. In the old church chest there was a "terrier," which sets forth the manner in which tithes were to be paid in kind. In addition to the tithe of wheat there was also one of wool, and the manner of tithing it was this :—

The owner lays his whole year's produce in five parcels or heaps. The vicar, or person employed by him, chuseth one of the five heaps, which he pleases, and divides the same into two parts, of which two parts the owner chuses the one, and leaves the other to the vicar for the tenth part. Also the tithe of lambs in their proper kind throughout the parish, and the custom concerning them is this. If a person's number is one he pays a penny, if two he pays twopence, and so on until five, then he pays half a lamb ; if six he pays a whole lamb, the vicar paying back fourpence ; if seven threepence, if eight twopence ; if nine a penny ; after the vicar hath a lamb complete. And in like manner for every number above ten. And if a man's number is under fifty, the tithe taken is this : The owner takes up two, then the vicar takes one, next the owner takes nine, then again the vicar one, and so on until he hath taken the number due to him. If they are fifty or upwards they are put into a place together and run out singly through a hole or gap ; the two first that come out are the owner's, the third the vicar's ; then the owner has the next nine, then the vicar one, and so on until the vicar has his number. And if sheep are sold in the spring, the tithe of lambs is paid by the person with whom they are lambed, whether seller or buyer. The tithe of geese throughout the parish, taken up about Michaelmas yearly, in the same manner as lambs, except that where a penny is paid on the account of each odd lamb, a halfpenny is paid for each odd goose. Also the tithe of pigs throughout the parish in like manner; also the tithe of eggs about Easter; two eggs for each old hen and duck, and one egg for each chicken and duck of the first year; also by each person who sows hemp is paid annually one penny; also for each plough is paid yearly one penny; also for every person keeping bees is paid one penny; also an oblation of sixpence for every churching of women. . . . Also for every person of age to communicate, three-halfpence due at Easter. There is also due to the parish clerk for every family in the parish keeping a separate fire three-halfpence yearly, and for every proclamation in the churchyard twopence.

It will be seen that almost everything which the dalesfolk possessed was subject to tithing, but I am bound in justice to my grandfather to say that he was charitable in the levying of it, and in many cases only insisted upon the payment of such a small portion as to secure his right to collect. There are one or two matters in this list which I should like to mention, and I may also say that the "terrier" which sets forth the above, we one wet afternoon disinterred from a parcel of musty manuscripts in an old oaken chest which had long stood in the vestry of my father's church. It will be seen that part of the limited income of the clerk was obtained by the various proclamations he was accustomed to make from the church porch. He told of sales of peat and

bacon, of farming stock, and of all those matters information of which is now furnished by notices on the church doors. The parish clerk was a great man in old church times, as

I shall shortly have to set forth. One of my grandfather's clerks happened to be a country shoemaker by trade, and he invariably brought to church a capacious blue wallet in which to collect "repairs." And it was not unusual to see the old clergyman sitting on a tombstone before service commenced, conning over these, and suggesting a "speck" here and a "patch" there, or whatever seemed best. The repository for these was a hollow oak which stood at the bottom of the churchyard; this was blown down in a storm on a Christmas day fifty years ago.

CHAPTER II.

IF we happened to have had a good hay harvest, and the mows filled the barns to bursting, we were allowed to play in my father's church on wet days or when snowed in. It was upon one of these occasions that we discovered in the vestry the massive oaken chest, which we found to contain a great pile of parish documents. Many of these were old and weather-stained, and dated back centuries. The chest was carved out of the solid trunk of an oak, and the yellow parchments could not have been in safer keeping. These documents gave us almost a new interest in life, and subsequently we spent many wintry afternoons in deciphering their contents. It was from among these that we came to know of the manner of tithing when tithe was paid in kind. This has already been set forth. In addition to the levying of these there were "Easter Dues" to pay according to the following table. It will be seen that the article comes first in order then a contraction of the same in Latin, and lastly the amount :—

Smoke, *fum.*, 1d. ; garden, *hort.*, ½d., and a gentleman's, 1d. ; apples, *pom.*, 1d. ; bees, *apes*, ½d. each swarm till the fifth, then 1s. 6d., 1s. 10d., and in like proportion ; milk, *lac.*, 1½d. ; calves, *vit.*, ½d. each till five, then as in order above ; plough, *arat.*, 1d.; ploughing for hire, 2d. Item, for a sermon on Ascension Day from the Chamber of B——, yearly, 10s. ; hemp, *canal*, ½d. ; flax, ½ *linum*, 1d.; mire meadow, *fœnum*, 1d. per acre ; geese, *ans.*, 2d.; colt, *pul.*, 1d. till five, then as above ; chickens, *pul. gal.*, 1d.; and eggs in kind ; swine, *porc.*, 1d. each till ve, then half a pig 9d., and a whole pig in like proportion, &c.

Documents which we were unable to understand we were wont to take into the house to have their contents explained, and it was then we first learned that our mother neither approved the paying of tithes nor Easter dues—that her people had always resisted them, and had borne their testimony against them. She would not allow that a tithe upon the produce of the earth and upon the increase of the fields was a divine institution, at least in our time, and without cavilling or casting reflections upon any she lost no suitable opportunity of supporting her testimony to my father that tithes were an anti-Christian yoke. Easter dues she protested against in like manner, as demands originally made by the Church of Rome, but continued for services which, speaking for herself, she could not accept. The views which my mother took on these subjects are strongly impressed upon my memory, and with good reason. For anything in the nature of a disagreement in our home was so rare, that certain occasions stand out vividly from a rather colourless background. At these times my mother was most becoming in what she said and in her manner of saying it; but she was a woman of such strong convictions and quick intellect that she always spoke out clearly and well what she thought at the time. My father again had much sympathy with her, but still went his way, as became a clergyman of the Established Church. Indeed, he had reason to sympathise with her, as she had borne much for him. I say this because the Society of Friends have a deep-rooted objection to marriage by a priest, thinking it inconsistent with their testimony to the true nature and character of the marriage ordinance. From this it will be seen that from the view of the early Friends my mother in her marriage committed a double fault, for she was not only married by a priest, but to a priest. She told me in after life that she well knew what she incurred by so doing, but that still she married my father advisedly, and that the latter's love and kindness to her during their time of courtship had only proved an earnest of what she had experienced through her life. The last admonition she had before entering the church in her simple Quaker costume was from Isaac Wilson, an old friend and an elder. He said, "Whilst people differ in religious views, they stand disunited in the main point—even that which should increase and confirm their mutual happiness, and render them helps to each other."

As yet I have only spoken of the primitive church life in the valley, and have said but little of that of the people. The living of 1780 presented a striking contrast with that of to-day. It was then that a great revolution in the manners and customs of the people took place. Much that was singular and characteristic among them vanished at the opening of the turnpike roads. These afforded them opportunities for the purchase of objects of comfort, even of elegance, and produced results which soon spread to the more secluded mountain dales. The tracks of the pack horses were difficult for travellers at all times, and as a rule they were ill kept. Personal intercourse with the southern portions of the country was then difficult. We speak lightly now of the will-making of our fore-elders before starting on a long journey, but to them this was a matter of no small consideration, and those whose business took them from home settled their worldly affairs before starting. Many of these were small manufacturers of woollen goods, having small mills on the mountain streams.

Their goods they sometimes travelled to sell, conveying their merchandise on the backs of pack-horses. With the macadamised roads the strings of pack-horses began to decline, and post-chaises were introduced. Soon after this carriers' carts and wagons came in, and a tale began to be told in the dales by one who had seen it, that a stage-coach had begun to run from Edinburgh to London, passing the foot of the valley on its way, and the marvellous part of the story was that this "flying machine" took but fourteen days for the journey. Older people shook their heads doubtingly at the enterprise, and some of the learned doctors warned people from travelling by the wild and whirling vehicle, as the rate at which it went would bring upon them all manner of strange disorders, chief among which was apoplexy. This was only the beginning, however, of many and rapid changes. Then, spinning wheels were in every hill farm, and the cloth which the dalesfolk wore was homespun. Outside the domestic circle a few hand-loom weavers wove cloth of duffel grey for the men and russet for the use of the women. Finer wool for finer work was carefully combed within the settle nook, but almost all for domestic use. The woolcomber was a great

man in those days, and the itinerant who tramped the country and turned wooden dishes and such-like articles was always received kindly. These men were the news carriers of the times, and it was from among them, some years later, that our neighbour, Mr Wordsworth, drew the character of his immortal "Wanderer." The produce of the flax-field yielded material for holiday attire, and it was in great request amongst women. In those days the travelling tailor went from house to house in search of employment, and in the larger of them was sometimes detained for weeks. He worked for daily wages, and amply paid for his meat and drink by the news he brought. Although the home produce was large, money was scarce, and the earnings of the servants were paid "in kind." The girls received shifts and gowns and aprons; the men shirts and coats, with sometimes a little wool and corn. In money the annual wages of a man-servant would have been about £5, of a woman £2. In our old hill church there is a fine mural monument to Dame Gylpine, of the Hall. I have before me an account of "the holle yeare waigs of all her servants at S——," and these amount to 290s. for eight men and nine "maydes." In the days of Dame Gylpine (about fifty years before the time of which I am speaking) a thorough knowledge of domestic art was considered necessary to fit a lady for the duties of wife and mother. Where one woman can knit a pair of stockings now there were a hundred then, though in the matters of music and philosophy the proportion is reversed. And in these bygone days, even the country gentle-folk deemed it no degradation to manage their own affairs down to the minutest details.

I am glad to say that my mother encouraged us, especially my sister Rachel, in all the little home arts, and we proved proficients in many of them. Our work with the wool I shall have to speak of later, and it was this that provided our chief indoor labour and employment during the long winter evenings.

From what I know of the old parish chest already mentioned, I cannot but think that there is much valuable history like to that which it contains which has not yet seen the light. I am bound to confess that in times past the clergy were very careless of these treasures, and did nothing to preserve them. Their worst enemies would seem to have been mice and damp. Fortunately, those in my father's church were in the bowels of an oak tree as it were, and have not suffered much. Then the walls of the church were of such extraordinary thickness that damp could never penetrate them, and I am pleased to say that most of the chest documents can be easily deciphered. Of these I intend to say a little here, and also to give some specimens. I have already set forth several of these ancient manuscripts on tithes and Easter dues, and the manner in which they were levied. Among the more interesting documents were the churchwardens' books. It appears from entries in these, that upon the occasion of the "letting out" of a family the churchwardens spent not stintingly in liquor. They also "loosed goods out of pawn," and I find an entry of two shillings for "seeing Ann Andie through her confinement," and another of ninepence for "cloggs for Aggie Todd's bastard." This last entry reminds me that illegitimacy was one of the commonest evils in the dales a century ago, and was perhaps owing to the very imperfect domestic arrangements, more especially in farm houses.

Another entry in one of the books is to the effect that John Wilson be paid at the rate of £5 for his first two years of mole-catching, and £2 annually afterwards. The number of ravens' heads for which the church-wardens paid is great, as many as twelve having been received at one time. These were fastened to the door of the church, as were the feet of the marten, weasel, otter, badger, stoat, foumart, carrion crow, &c. The vicar paid 3d. for the head of a raven, 6d. for that of a fox or a badger, 3d. for that of a marten, and 1d. each for the smaller vermin. Another frequent item in the books is that of strewing the floor with rushes, 2s. 6d. "Ringing the year" seems to have been a regular institution, this being done at Christmas and Easter. A penny is the price for making and setting the dial post, remains of which still exist in the churchyard. A "constable" received annual payment, and needy wayfarers were frequently relieved. At the "hanging of the belle" much money was spent in liquor, and the clerk's wages amounted to sixteen shillings a year. Other contents of the chest are wills, of which there are many, some of them strangely curious as to their contents. The one following, dated 1542, is that of a tanner. Tanning, even three centuries ago, was almost the only trade of a neighbouring valley, and it was practised by a few families just at the estuary of the Greenwash. Here is the will of Edmunde Persone—

In Dei nomine, Amen. The xxjth daye off Decembre, in the yere off oure Lorde Gode a thousande fyv hundrethe forty and two, I, Edmunde Persone, off the parishynge off C——, tannere, hol of mynde and off gud remembrance, seke and craiysed . . . and wote not when God will call me to his mercye, maketh my laste wylle and testamente in maner and fourme folowying. Fyrst, I gyve and bewhethithe my sowle unto Almighty God, and to oure blessed Ladye Saynte Marye, and to all the holy company of hevyn, and my body to be buried within my parish churche of B——, before the ymage of our Ladye. Also it is my wylle that the said churche shall have all it duties accustomede. Item; I give and bewheth mye hole tityll and tenandright of my howse and farmhold with all the appurtenannce thereto belongynge in W——, aftere my decesse, unto Thomas

Borrowe, sone into mye doughter Mabelle, with my barkhouse and the instruments thereto belongynge. Also I wylle that Edwarde Borrowe, brothere to the saide Thomas, have his father's place lying at the Storthe, with the licence off the lorde, after the decesse of my saide doughter Mabelle. Also it is my wyll that such a sowme of goods as I have named unto Sire Richard Dykonson, vicare of the said B——, Sir Henry Ayraye, Richard Bradegate, Waltere Kendalle, and Edwarde Symson, shal be geven unto a stokker at my saide parishe church, towarde the fyndynge off a preste for to teche a free scole, and to praye for my sawle and all christen sawles. Also it is my wyll that iiij. nowbills of the sayd sowme shal ne geven to praye for my sonnes saule, Miles Persone, and other iiij. nowbills of ye same sowme, to be for the saule off Robert Newbye to be prayed for also. Also it is mye wyll to make the cost off the mason warke to the supportacione and makynge of a brigge at the end of M——. Also I gyve to the mendynge of the cawsere betwix S—— and brigge. . . . Also I gyve unto the mendynge of the gutture in Melood chancelle, vjs. viijd. Also it is my wylle . . . siche guds as I bave *gevne* to a stoke to ye fyndynge of a preste at the chapell of our Lady on ye . . . in ye W——, shal remayne to the same porpose forever. Also I ordeyne and makethe my right . . . full Ladye Anne Aeshton, Petere Crosfield, and Waltere Kendalle my hole executors, and Edward ——, all the reste off my goodes that doth remayne from . . . whethes and gifts shall be disposed at the sight and discretione of my said executors, for the helth of my sawle. Also I wylle that the said Edward Symson and Thomas Borrowe resave the said sowme gevyn to . . . stak at B—— by me and shall receive it at my hande and be orderers and as hids for me and latters furth of the same, as is more largely shewed in a writynge bering date hereofe. Item, I make John Martyndalle —— Masborowe the supervisors of this my last will and testament, to se yt it be well & truly fulfilled an kepid . . . true intent. The witnesse heroff, Sire Richarde Dykonson, Sir Henry Ayraye, Richard Bradegate with other mo, & specially William Peper & Thomas Grubye.

This is ye Inventarye of the goods of Edmunde Persone of W——, latlye decessed, on whose saule God have mercye, seyne & prised by John Matyndales, Thomas Peper, William Peper, & Thomas Grubye, on the iiijth day of Januarye in the xxxiiijth yere of the reygne of Kynge Henrye the vijth. Fyrst, so many sheipe olde and zinge as cometh to ye valew of v. marks. And by farther knawlege we fyndmo yt cometh to the valew of xiijs. iiijd. Also we fynde shepe of ane other . . . to ye valew of xlljs. iiijd. Also we have seyn such beddying and insyght as was in the howse and an olde horse yt cometh to ye valew of xxxiijs. iiijd. Also so muche ledes in ye lymme pytts as draweth xix marks, vjs. viijd. *Debeta quæ ei debentur.* Primis, Maistres Curwen, when sche was widow at H——, xls. Item, Jamis Robynson of Crostewhat, xlvs. Item, Mils Symkynson, xxxvs. viijd., and my will is yt he be easelye dalte with all. Item, William Crossfelde, vjs. viijd. Thomas Banke, xiijs. Edwarde Kylners wyf, iiijd. Thomas Banke xiijs. Edwarde Kylners wyf, ijs. Miles

Deconson, xxvs. Henry Sherman, vs. iiijd., which he tok up at M——. Nycolas Crathom, vs., whiche the said Henry Sherman toke up. Thomas Browne, xixs. vijd. Miles Knype, xijs. George Mason of D——, xxviijs. iiijd. Leonarde Waller, xls. James Striclande, iijs. One Bone of L——, vjs. viijd. Also there was spendyde at his buryall, to ye church dutye, to the priests and clarkes, and for the dinner, xls. Also ye expenses at was made in his house, while he layde, and at his wawke, xvjs., whiche the saide Edmunde saide shulde be paide with his awn gudes. Also vjs. viijd. to Jenette Loremere late his servante.

CHAPTER III.

I REMEMBER two parish clerks in connection with our old hill church, which is a privilege not given to most men. These important items of parish rule are generally long-lived, and how I come to have known two is that one of them was a very old man when I was a boy, and he lived to a great age. Dalesfolk invariably do. Upon this I would remark, that although Italian skies might prevail generally, our poor hill parish seemed to be perpetually under a cloud. And yet, in spite of life being spent in cold mists, the dwellers in the dale attained to a ripe old age. This was peculiarly so with parish clerks. In their number of days these worthies seemed to treat the orthodox threescore years and ten with a lofty contempt, and some of the people openly expressed themselves to the effect that this was a mistranslation. To attempt to describe these ancient pieces of anatomy would convey but general ideas. In the dales even now they are occasionally met with, and seem to be carved out of the tree of life. Many of them live years beyond their share, and a few can recount the history of a century. To come, however, from a class to an individual:—

> The Bible says the age o' man
> Threescore and ten perchance may be.
> He's ninety-eight. Let them wha' can
> Explain the incongruity.
> He should ha' lived afore the flood,
> He's come o' patriarchal blood,
> He's some auld pagan mummified,
> For further continuity.

In short, a young parish clerk is as rare as a Quaker baby. Those known to us boys were old, very old. At least they always seemed so, and I do not think that it ever once struck us that they were once young like ourselves. By some strange combination of circumstances, the parish clerk was either a shoemaker or a tailor. And yet he was never modest. Matthew Mould was a shoemaker; but then he always kept the "little shop," was postmaster, registrar, and chief constable. He used to stumble over the personal names in the Psalms in a manner that was alarming, but no one ever suggested that he was ignorant. His predecessor, R. G., "surgeon, parish clerk, and schoolmaster,"

"Reforms ladies and gentlemen that he draws teeth without waiting a moment—blisters on the lowest terms, and fysicks at a penny. Sells Godfather's cordial, cuts corns, and undertakes to keep anybody's nails by the year or so on. Young lades and gentelmen tort their grammer language in the neatest possible manner; also grate care taken of their morals and spellin; also sarme singing and teaching the Ho, boy, cow Tillions and other dances tort at home and abroad. Perfumery in all its branches. Sells all sorts of stationery wares, black balls, red herring, and coles. Scrubben brushes, trecle, mouse traps, and all other sort of sweetmeats; taters, sassages, and other garden stuffs; also frute, hats, ballits, novel, tinware, and other eatables. Turnner sarve, corn sarve, and all hardwares. He also performs fleebottomy in a curious manner, old rags bought and sold here, not any ware helse, and new-laid eggs every day. . . . P.S. I teeches joggrefy and all them outlandish things. N.B. A bawl on Wednesday."

Matthew Mould, my father's clerk, rose above his contemporaries in the matter of learning. He knew everything, and was consulted by everybody; and in the person of this worthy was carried about the unwritten history of the place. Like another Toby Wilt, he was on friendship with the bells, and, we used to think, with the bats and owls that frequented the belfrey. Once daily for fifty long years he climbed the stone steps to wind up the quaint clock in the tower, and, like the famous prisoner of Chillon, he has left his footprints on the stairs. In church, Matthew occupied the lowest tier of the "three-decker," which was surmounted by a sounding board. Before service commenced he used to hang out a blackboard over the edge of the gallery, on which was inscribed the number of the psalms we were to sing that day. Then, as service progressed, he gave out the psalm from the desk. He held a pitch-pipe in his hand, and blew a sepulchral note out of it, as the key-note of the tune. As one of the worshippers has said; this was done with a dismal sort of flourish to the nasal monotone in which he read out the words, for the sake of illustration running as follows :—

O, 'twas a joyful sound to hear
Our tribes devoutly say—Too, Too.

The singers took up the note and off they went, with bassoon and clarionct accompani-

ment, to one of those grand old tunes which requires the last two lines to be sung in fractional parts, and ends in a comprehensive bang, in which everybody, vocalists and instrumentalists, come in together at the finish. They had parted company early in the proceedings. Excruciating melodies those tunes were, the composition for the most part of parish clerks. At the hill church the *Nunc Dimittis* used to be sung to an arrangement of "O Lady Fair," with variations only as regarded time. There was also a version of "My mother bids me bind my hair," as a common measure, with quite ingenious alliteration. Although the parish clerks of the hill churches were ignorant, they were by no means modest, for once when the minister had lost his way in the Communion Service, he was called to order by the clerk vociferating, "Ye've missed 'pistle." Upon occasion it has always been, and is even now, in winter, customary in time of snow to have a short service if there be only four or five worshippers, and then to adjourn to the vestry, where there is usually a turf fire. At these times parish affairs are discussed, and the men-folk have sometimes gone so far as to have the added comfort of tobacco. It was rarely, however, that service was altogether abandoned, and the ecclesiastical procedure set down below is perhaps without a precedent. It happened in one of the hill dales, and the church in which it occurred is located to this day. Upon one memorable occasion the clerk gave notice to the assembled worshippers to the following effect—" There'll be nae service in this church for m'appon a matter o' fower weeks, as parson's hen is sitting in t' pulpit."

I have said that one of our parish clerks among his other offices held that of chief constable. There was but little of ill-doing in the dale, but when a rare malefactor was taken in his wickedness it fell to the lot of the clerk to convey his prisoner to one of the northern gaols. He was always charitably disposed, however, and to show this, and his topographical knowledge, he invariably conducted his prisoner about the town, so that he might not lose his way when liberated. To his lot upon another occasion it fell to execute a writ of *fieri facias* on a doctor. The latter spied him coming, and, like Penn of old, barricaded the premises. Finding persuasion and cajolery of no avail to gain admission, he tried the strength of legal authority. "I demand," cried he, "admittance under the Act of the Fiery Furnace." How far the terrible threat succeeded is not known. The same clerk never passed the communion rails without bobbing his head, just as the old women who came to church always curtesied in the same act. Everybody turned to the east at the creed, though not one of them, including the clerk, exactly knew why.

There was one custom in these old church days which had a strong hold upon the people, and which lingers in the hill parishes yet. All the female part of the congregation who came to afternoon service carried their prayer books (they were innocent of print) in their handkerchiefs. In addition to this they had a bit of "suttering wood," and a small packet of strong mint lozenges. They would as soon have thought of attending church without these fetishes as without their Sunday gowns.

I well remember a university friend being brought to book by our parish clerk. My father had invited the former to take part in the service, as was his wont when clerical friends visited us. If I remember aright, it was one of the first occasions my friend had officiated, and in his nervousness he gave out the wrong day of the month before singing morning psalms. This the old man detected immediately. He looked up and said, "Nay, parson, yer wrang howiver, it's t' day after." Matthew always spoke in the broadest dialect, and before service, after sounding on his pitch-pipe, he would walk up the aisle, repeating, "Let's begin t' worship o' God wi' singin' t' Morning Hymn;" and the choir, worshippers, and clerk would bang away at "Awake my soul and with the sun," &c.

I have already said something of the quaintness of the parish clerks of our own church and of those belonging to the neighbouring valleys, but if these were characters in their own way, they were admirably kept in countenance by many of the old clergymen who were my grandfather's contemporaries. In a certain northern coast village, for instance, it was the custom to despoil the wreckage when vessels were driven ashore. Here upon the beach there stood a quaint old church which often served as a morgue, for the drifting sandbanks of these seas were a Charybdis to the coast mariners, and as many as twenty-five bodies have been laid out in the little church at one time. During service there rushed in one Sunday morning an excited parishioner with the news that a well-laden vessel had been driven ashore. The members of the congregation were immediately on their feet and rushing towards the doors, when their pastor appealed to them in solemn tones: "Brethren," said he, "let's start fair," and with that he bolted out of the vestry door. I have heard it said that this parson and his flock almost lived on wreckage, and were by no means particular as to how they caused it. The church here was entirely without drapery, and the parson's surplice hung over a desk where he had last doffed it. The graves in the churchyard were in clusters, and those buried were of almost every nationality. To pass on to a practice which prevailed in the same district—not in the hill country, but at a then fishing village—not long ago either, it may be mentioned that it was the wont of the clerk to announce, just before the Litany, the sales of agricultural produce which were likely to take place during the current week—a bit of ritual likely to alarm latter-day worshippers. In fact, I am afraid these announcements were of as much importance as the sermon to some, and of more to others. But our old church folk are fast dying out, and with them their practices; so that the descendants of the hill parishes to-day, instead of proclaiming these mundane things from the second tier of a three-decker, simply affix a notice to the like effect on the church door, the said document often consisting of words and phrases fearfully and wonderfully made.

A parallel to my grandfather in some

respects — though I am afraid more worldly-minded—was a stout hill clergyman who was a great authority on cattle. He was a regular attender and one of the best known figures at the fortnightly fair, and here he might be seen poking cattle in the ribs, and valuing them. Upon these occasions he was dressed in a long black coat, drab breeches and gaiters, and he invariably carried a big stick. Later in the day he might be seen in the village alehouse, surrounded by his brother bucolics, smoking a long clay pipe, and drinking beer. Being asked once how he found time to compose his sermons, he said that he had never made one out of his own head for thirty years. "I give my folk Tillotson," said he, "and what can you find better?" He was a learned antiquary, however, as was the case with many of the old country clergy, and it is said that he could recite the title to every estate for miles around, and knew the parish boundaries to an inch. The old man died many years ago of a cold caught on the wintry moors in crossing to visit a dying woman. This reverend man being (and of necessity) much interested in farming pursuits, it is not extraordinary that one Sunday, before commencing service, he leant over the edge of the pulpit and said to a parishioner in a loud whisper—"Have ye seen owt o' two hill sheep o' mine; they're smitten i' t'ear like yours, but deeper i' smit?" This man was one of that class of clergy who had to farm their glebe land so as to make both ends meet, and being in a hill district had a run for sheep upon the common, which was then without fences and unenclosed. A neighbour of ours, a clergyman, who was somewhat eccentric, but who possessed strong common sense, found upon one occasion when he had mounted the pulpit that he had forgotten his sermon. He felt in all his pockets for his missing manuscript, but failing to find it he said that if the people did not mind he would read them a chapter from the book of the prophet Job, remarking that this was worth at least the best six sermons that he had ever written. No one objected, and the good old man read the chosen chapter to the good of all. Miss

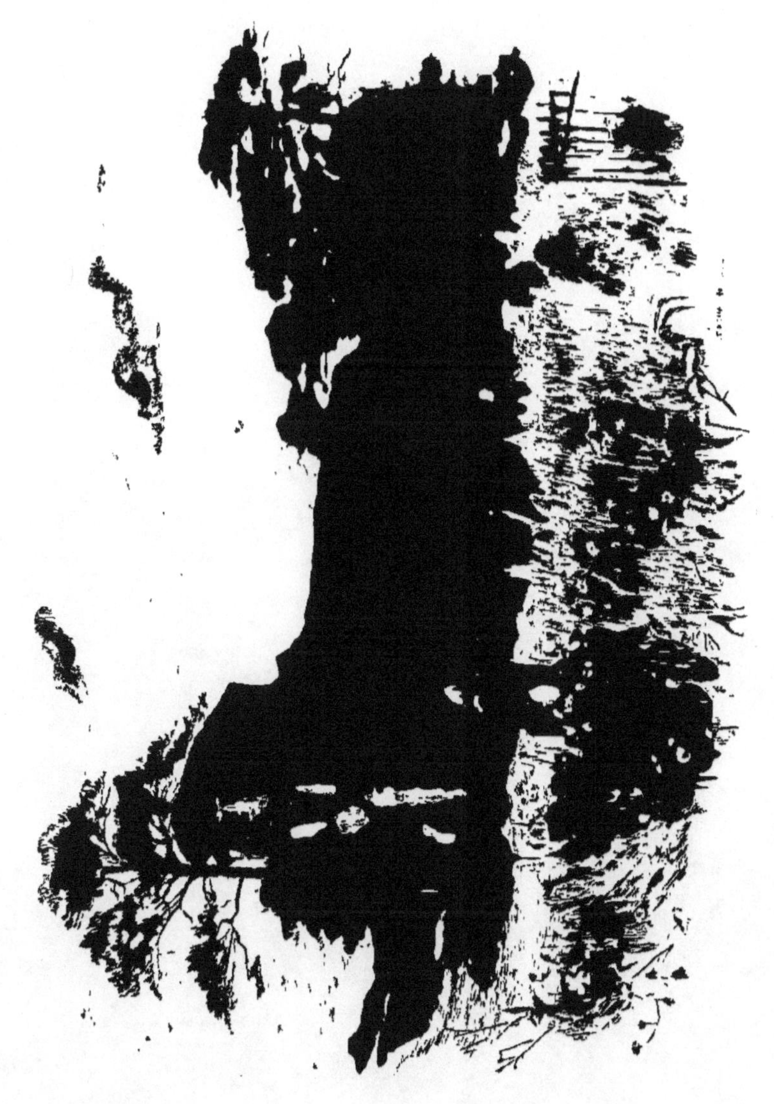

Martineau was fond of relating an anecdote of a hill parson who could get through the church service in a shorter time than any of his neighbours. He would give any living clergyman a start as far as some portion, which he indicated, and then he would beat him in the end.

For many years the church at L—— was without a door, with the consequence that in rough weather the cattle used to take advantage of it as a "bield" or shelter, by reason of which it was not unfrequently polluted. To prevent this a large thorn bush was dragged into the doorway. After service (the parson of course leaving by the vestry door) it was generally understood that the last who left the church was to place the thorn *in situ*, the parson going round to see fair play, and to act as referee if necessary.

At the church where this took place, from the terribly severe hills among which it lies, service was probably more frequently omitted than elsewhere in the whole of the Lake group of mountains. And if the snow happened to be exceptionally heavy, and there were but few present at the administration of the Holy Communion, the clergyman used to whisper to those kneeling at the rails, "Drink gayly deep; there's not many o' us this morning." Where this occurred the clerk had the strongest pair of lungs in the country-side; he could not only drown the parson's voice, but that of the assembled congregation, and he did it too. Here it used to be the custom to hold wrestling matches in the Church Field, and to indulge in various games of prowess. When the bell had tolled for the "last time," the young yeomen would don their coats, jump over the wall, and come filing into church, spitting on their hands to smooth down their rebellious hair.

In a neighbouring parish, one Annas Jackson, for some sin of her frail nature, had to do penance in her girlhood by walking barefoot through the church in a white sheet. This garment was afterwards suspended behind the vestry door, and was once put on by a stranger clergyman who had come to officiate. Remarking its soiled appearance to the clerk, he was told to take it off, as it was "old

Anna's penance sheet." In still another dale the inhabitants were in the habit of going out hunting on Sundays. Their Sabbath breaking and lawlessness became so flagrant that the parson openly denounced them from the pulpit, and said, "O, ye wicked of W——, if you go a-hunting any more on the Sabbath day, I'll go with you," and the clergyman, being as fond of hunting as the rest, kept his word and went. Parish feeling runs strongly now-a-days, but not more so than in old times, as the following incident will show. An impressive sermon was preached, and all were moved to tears, except one old man. Upon being remonstrated with, he said he didn't cry "because he didn't belong to the parish."

This church lore is of a past order of both men and things, only I have thought it well to preserve some of the healthiest anecdotes concerning them, and these may not prove uninteresting. Wrestling, spell and knur, pitch and toss, are now no longer played at the church door, and nearly all things in this connection have improved.

CHAPTER IV.

ANYONE who had visited our old hill church might have found what in Athens Diogenes sought in vain—an honest man, or at least the record of one. The graveyard was a strange, tumbledown place, and the stones scattered about were with homely rhymes and shapeless sculpture decked. The slab to which I particularly allude covered the sod whereunder lay the remains of one John Taylor, a yeoman. And anent it we are told—

> One truth o'er these remains below,
> More lasting honour will bestow
> Than lineage, wealth, or grandeur can—
> Here lies interred an honest man.

Down in a corner of the ground was a mound overgrown with docks and nettles. These covered the remains of a poor wayfarer whom we found one Christmas time on the fells dead and half buried with snow. He had nothing upon him by which he could be identified, and we buried him as decently as we could in the mountain churchyard, having to dig through the hard frosty ground to make his grave. Nobody cared for him in his new resting-place, and nature soon obliterated the spot with a covering of kindly mantling green. None of the surrounding stones were of much interest, though inside the church was a mural monument to Dame Gylpine, of the Hall, done in white marble. There was also one which bore the following curious epitaph:—

> A man I was, wormes meate I am,
> To earth returned from whence I came.
> Many removes on earth I had,
> In earth at length my bed is made;
> A bed which Christ did not disdaine,
> Although it could not him retaine,
> His deadlie foes might plainly see,
> Over sin and death his victorie.
> Here must I rest till Christ shall let me see
> His promised Jerusalem and her felicitie.

These lines were carved over the remains of a truly remarkable man, whom Sir Walter Scott has immortalised otherwhere. At the west end of the old church is the following inscription in a large wooden frame, in black characters on a gold ground:—

Here lyes Frances,
late wife of Jacob
Dawson, gent., who
departed this life 19
June 1700; in ye 25th year
of her age.
Who by a Free, and chearfull
resignation of herselfe
(even in the midst of
this world's affluence)
Has left us just grounds
to hope she is
now happy.

This epitaph has given rise in the dale to a witticism, used sometimes as a toast on particular occasions of festivity, viz., "May we all live as Jacob Dawson's wife died." The last inscription which I shall give as being of any general interest is that on a brass plate within the Communion rails, and is probably unique. It runs as follows; "Herevnder Lyeth ye Body of Mr Ravlph Tirer, Late Vicar of——, Batchler of Divinity, Who Dyed the 4th Day of Jvne, Ano; Dni: 1627."

London bredd me, Westminster fedd me,
Cambridge sped me, my Sister wed me,
Study taught me, Living sought me,
Learning brought me, K—— caught me,
Labour pressed me, sickness distressed me,
Death oppressed me, and grave possessed me,
God first gave me, Christ did save me,
Earth did crave me, and heaven would have me.

I shall leave this remarkable epitaph (which, as might be supposed, was written by the reverend gentleman himself) and pass on to other matters connected with our little church. To return to the graveyard, there was, standing slightly off the path, a quaint sun-dial, of a strange and curious make. This, however, was broken and tumbled, and had been superseded many years by the silver watches owned by the farmers. These were huge pieces of mechanism, and were carried in their owners' "fobs." They had also many dependent seals and curiously contorted scraps of metal attached, all of which gave dignity to the wearer. It was a sight to see these stalwart yeomen dive down into their capacious pockets and bring up watches. It entailed a struggle and a whole series of evolutions. The body was drawn up, the head thrown a little aside, whilst the great rubicund face twitched in every muscle the

while. But all this exertion went for something, for, once the watch was outside, the yeoman held it at arm's length before him,

and gazed upon it with a slow appreciative intelligence lasting several minutes, and when he had fathomed its meaning he let it drop slowly down again to its depths. Near the sun-dial was a large flat-topped blue cobble from the stream bed, from which the sales were announced by the clerk; and a "mounting-stone" of a like nature stood just outside the churchyard gate. In my grandfather's day pillions were in use, and although some of these survive among the lumber of the old barns, they are now rarely or never used.

Over the churchyard entrance was, and

still is, a "lich-gate." Many of the older country churches retain these, and by them hangs a history. They are remotely connected with the plague which ravaged these parts at an early period. No ancient document furnishes much concerning them, but one I found in the parish chest contained the following: "Plague was in P——and K——1554" (these being neighbouring parishes). From other sources, however, we know that this epidemic periodically devastated certain parts of the North, and that it visited this parish in 1384. Nearly two hundred years elapsed before another attack occurred, but in 1597 the terrible scourge again visited the dales, and almost depopulated some of them. In one parish alone, certainly a large one, 2500 of the inhabitants perished. In support of this the inscription here set down is confirmatory: "A.D. 1598, ex gravi peste quæ regionibus hisce incubuit obierunt, apud P——, 2,260, K——,2,500, R——, 2,200, C——, 1,160. Posteri vortite vos et vivite (1)." Now, it will be seen that during an infectious pestilence of this nature, personal communication between dwellers of different parts would be almost cut off. At first probably but few deaths occurred, and, to prevent contagion, corpses, instead of being taken into the church, were deposited on biers beneath the "lich-gate," where the service for the dead would be read. (Lich is the Saxon *litsh*, a dead body, a corpse. A "lichwake" was a watching near the dead; and "lichfield," the field of the dead bodies; the lich-owl was superstitiously supposed to foretell death.) At the period to which I refer, lich-gates were probably introduced, and have since been so called. Beneath them the corpses of those who had died in the plague were laid so as to incur less chance of spreading the disease by introducing them within the church. From that day they have come down to our own, and are even now common. The people who died of the plague were not buried in the usual burial grounds—the number precludes that idea. In the hill parishes there was not room for them, nor were there those to undertake the task. Whole families were carried off together, and the streets of the country towns remained silent. The sick were left to die unaided. Country people whose parishes had as yet escaped the plague hardly dared to venture within the precincts of the towns, and left the provisions which they brought to places agreed upon, whence they could be taken by the townspeople. The money with which these were purchased was deposited in a stone trough, containing some disinfecting liquid, and not until it had undergone this process would the farmers receive it in payment for their goods. But where in the parish was this burial place of the vast numbers who had died? For years I had been interested in the matter, and had tried hard to discover it, when one day, talking to an old dalesman, he referred to one of his inclosures as "Barrow Field." Here, I thought, was a clue, for the name alone was suggestive. "Barrow" signifies a burial place—a tumulus raised as a depository of the dead, a custom of the Saxons. From these early people the name "barrow" had been handed on and on, even to my old parishioner. One afternoon I walked there to view the spot, and found it in the last belt of cultivation, and half way up the fell side; it was also a considerable distance from the road—probably for protective reasons. The grass was green over all, and there were no extraordinary indications. The wall which surrounded it, however, had at some time remote been immensely thick, and there are remains of an ancient gateway. I thrust my stick into the turf, and everywhere met stone. Parts of the fence, which is roughly triangular, are peculiar, and unlike the surrounding one. Then we dug down, and found what we thought to be burnt clothing, and that is all we could ever find; nor is it likely that anything of importance will be further discovered.

Of the oaken chest in the vestry I have already spoken. So interesting are its quaint contents that it is really difficult to get away from them; and next to the Churchwardens' books, maybe the most interesting are the Parish Registers. These yellow-stained parchment documents constitute a form of literature I could never resist. In all the old churches of the hill valleys you may find them, for the most part in chests such as I have described—heavy and hoary with age. Wipe away the dusts of antiquity, and they contain a record of forgotten things—many of them wisely so—and transport you to a past existence which you have but dimly dreamed of in this. If you would take the advice of one who has grown grey in their research, you will "let the dead past bury its dead." Never invade a parish register in this north country otherwise than as a curiosity of literature. You are young, and dream that blue blood runs in your veins? Be it so. Or there is some vast fortune about to accrue to you, and you wish to gather up the scattered links? You have infinite faith in the respectability of your family? Then let that faith be an abiding one. But don't, we beseech you, seek to verify these things through a parish register. If you do, you will find that it contains one terrible moral—that we are essentially of the earth, earthy; that our fore-elders were like us, "but more so." After this fair warning, should you be so indiscreet, your dreams will be rudely shaken. You go to the register to clear up some little crotchet of family history.

You have taken it as an acknowledged fact, and make pretty sure of your ground in the pedigree as far back as your grandfather. It is possible, even, you may find your great-grandfather without further tripping. A generation back and you are getting a little muddled. The names cross curiously and become strangely confusing, until, turning over a few more leaves, you find yourself in a mighty maze and all without a plan. You vex your brain, and just in proportion as you do this you plunge further and further into the slough of despond. If you are of a candid nature, you frankly admit that one or more of your male ancestors never had a corporeal existence, and that those of which you had made sure have become strangely mixed with the plebeian throng. And what does it matter? For it is only a case of time, when we, like they, will sink with the passionless host and float down in obscurity's tide. You may fancy that this is caricature; but the utter abyss of confusion produced by parish registers, the utter void of that abyss when you plunge into it after one simple family fact, defies caricature.

You examine a page, for instance, as here before me, and find that out of the six entries five are illegitimate. And in the neighbouring parishes, past morality has been at about the same ebb. There are other untoward omissions in parish registers. And this especially refers to Cumbria. Many of our forefathers, instead of dying in an orderly and peaceable manner in their beds, as, indeed, becomes Christians living in a Christian country, often died in less pleasant and convenient places. A neighbour of mine acquaintance, whose family has been established in the valley for generations, assures me that until a comparatively recent period hardly one of his male ancestors died decently. "Put to death by order of the Warden of the Marches," "Killed by Robert Howard's men," "Hunted to death by dogges in the mosses," "Ordered that his head should be stuck on the walls of the Tower, and all such like unto him,"—these and other similar pleasantries were the only early records that he could ever find of the way in which the various members of his line went out of the world. Still he boasts of his pedigree.

"The grand old gardener and his wife smile at the claims of long descent;" and, it appears from the foregoing facts, so does dame Nature. Tennyson's deduction from all this is that "'tis only noble to be good," that "kind hearts are more than coronets, and simple faith than Norman blood." And the world lives to prove the truth of this philosophy every day.

In most hillside parishes, I regret to say, the registers and other documents have been more or less carelessly kept. Many of them, too, are lost; but so far as these are extant, copies are now deposited in the mother church of the diocese. In many cases where they remain, modern safes have been obtained for their better keeping; and consequently the less secure, though more characteristic, arks and chests have been relegated to the aerial regions of cobwebs, bats, owls, and bells. Since many occasions have arisen to prove the legal value of these ancient documents, Parliament has decreed their greater accuracy and protection. Official and ruled forms have now to be filled in, and there is little reason to fear that in future vestry fires will be lighted upon occasion with parish history.

I have already mentioned a tragic death, and, as might have been expected, such events are rare in the annals of the valley. And yet there is a somewhat parallel case which had so far slipped my memory. The story is shortly told by a stone in a retired part of the churchyard, and reads as follows :—" Erected by an afflicted father to commemorate the memory and death of our only son, who . . . upon his return from K—— was waylaid and shot dead by a daring assassin, and his money taken from him, in a solitary lane not far from his own door. . . . He was cut down as a flower in the thirty-second year of his age. By his loss an endearing wife and three children were bereft of their kind parent. What is now unknown the judgment day will reveal." Fortunately such tales as this stone unfolds have been rare. The murderer, I believe, was never brought to justice, though a man living in the neighbourhood was long detained on suspicion. He had upon the night of the murder borrowed a double-barrelled gun from a neighbour.

Anent this incident I append from my notebook a scrap of homely tragedy. It runs as follows:—"None but those who have been caught in them can form any idea of how terrible are mountain snowstorms. Blinding, bewildering, both men and animals quickly succumb to them. Clouds and banks of snow rush hither and thither in opaque masses; the bitter hail and sleet seem to drive through you. A few moments after the storm breaks every wrap at command is soaked through, the cold is intense, and a sense of numbness soon takes possession of the whole body. Twice have I narrowly escaped death when out on the northern mountains in winter, suddenly finding myself at the close of a short afternoon enveloped in a blinding storm. Once, after long exposure, I owed my deliverance to a search party of shepherds; on the second occasion I was saved by the intelligent fidelity of a brace of foxhounds. Those who have been overtaken in this manner have not always been so fortunate; and some terrible deaths have occurred among the higher hills in winter. Half way down this grey stone wall on its near side is a sad green spot, and beside it we have thrown up a loose cairn. The snow had fallen thickly for many days; all the deep holes were filled up, and the mountain road was no longer to be seen. The wall tops stood out as white ridges on the otherwise smooth surface. Only the crags hung in shaggy snowy masses, black seams and scaurs picking out the ravines. Nature was sombre and still; it seemed as though her pulse had ceased to beat. The softly winnowed snowflakes still fell, and not even the wing of a bird of prey moved in the cold thin air. It had gone hard with the sheep. Hundreds were buried in the snow, and would have to be dug out. They sought the site of the old wall and fell into deep drifts; but the hardy goat-like herdwicks instinctively climbed to the bleak and exposed fell tops, and in this was their safety. To relieve the sheep that had as yet escaped, hay was carried to the fells, each shepherd having a loose bundle upon his back. It was thus, with three dogs, that we toiled up the gorge by an undefined trail parallel to the buried fence. Soon it began to snow heavily, and the sky suddenly darkened. The dogs that were in front stopped before some object. They whined, ran towards us, and gave out short, sharp barks. With a kind of instinctive dread we followed them as they led us towards a granite boulder, and on its lea side lay something starkly outlined against the snow. 'Dead'—we whispered to each other. There was no trace of pain over the features—nothing but rigid quiet. The icy fingers grasped a pencil, and on the snow lay a scrap of paper. It contained only two words—'This day'—then stopped. We buried the body next morning in the little mountain cemetery. Whence he came or whither he was going none ever knew. A few of the dead man's belongings, trifling enough, are thrust in a hole in the old barn for *her* whom we still expect to come for them one of these days."

CHAPTER V.

IN recording these annals, I have as yet spoken only of those things which centred about the church, and have so far left out the many incidents in the lives of the statesmen and yeomen. But these were neither few nor (at least some of them) of little import. There were frequently occurring matters of pleasantry, or grave or gay, which formed pleasing interludes in our otherwise quiet life. And although these were always welcomed when they arrived, yet the honest labour in the dale, and the willing efforts put forth to make the valley yield up its fruits, was that which was productive of the most lasting and real happiness. Marriages in country churches to-day are little more than solemn civil contracts; but in the dales a century ago they constituted occasions of general festivity. If the mountain church boasted a bell (and some of them possessed three) it rang out right merrily. The couple were escorted to the church by a group

of laughing neighbours, all decked out in pretty homespun, and bedizened with ribbons. But the bride herself! What shall be said, or not said, of her? She resembled Goldsmith's Bet Bouncer, and had cheeks broad and red as a parson's cushion. She had large true-blue bows across the full of her breast, lessening by degrees till they reached the waist. There was no "forsaken green" about the glad throng, nothing but bright blue, and white, and red. The parson always gave good advice to the couple after the wedding, telling them that they would go through life together, and that the great secret of happiness was that they should pull together. After the ceremony the bell rang more merrily than before, and there was loud kissing, and romping, and laughing. The native blush of the girls' cheeks was heightened to the colour of the hill heather, and the young men seemed strung on wire. Everybody and everything was full of lifeful activity. And now was practised a quaint custom which has long since died out. When the wedding party was well outside the church a dozen youths would pull off their shoes and stockings, and reveal the fact that their legs were begirt with parti-coloured ribbons. They would then range themselves in line, until a word from the bride started them off to her house in what was among the yeomen "a race of kisses." The competitors rushed away to the encouraging shouts of the spectators, the victor returning to meet the bride and blushingly ask for his prize—a kiss and a ribbon. Festivity was kept up until daybreak on the following morning, when all would separate to their homes. It must be remembered that these primitive festivities were held in a valley that at the time of which I write was practically cut off from the world, and when it was said that but one chaise had been known to visit it. And yet almost perfect contentment was enjoyed here, where everything grew in the minds of the dalesfolk and became a necessary part of them. One simple philosopher was wont to say, "My father, grandfather, and great-grandfather farmed and fished yon tarn, and I would not leave the place for the world." Time out of mind, almost, the country children had been taught to dance, and the dancing-master was as important a personage and much more common than the schoolmaster. This popular art was taught in the spacious barns of the yeomen, and the elders, who stood aloof as spectators, were as much interested in the proceedings as the children. They ranged themselves round the barn, and watched with evident delight. Hornpipes and cotillons were the dances most in repute, but, of whatever kind, they were incomplete without the strains of a fiddle, which in many cases was played by the dancing-master himself. Most of the barns of the farmers had suspended in the centre a wooden hoop, with tin sockets for candles, so as always to be ready of an evening for a dance. Although these people loved their festal days, there was a meritorious spirit of industry among them, and the women spent most of their time in knitting and spinning. Coal was not as yet used in the country districts as fuel, nor is it now to any extent; but when turf had been brought from the moorlands the women carted it into the neighbouring villages to sell in the shape of peats.

With regard to dress I have already referred

to homespun ; but I should like to mention the ironshod shoes, called "clogs," which were very generally worn half a century ago. The parson's and the yeoman's children invariably appeared in them at church on Sundays. These clogs proved terribly injurious to the wearer's stockings, and careful housewives used to smear the heels with melted pitch and dip them immediately in the ashes of a turf fire. Fixed in the woollen texture, the mixture became both hard and flexible, and was well adapted to resist friction. Flax has long ceased to be grown in the field ; there is now no hempen cloth, and the old methods of spinning have gone out. Into some of the northern valleys, Mr Ruskin—striving after an unattainable ideal of pastoral peace and happiness—has re-introduced spinning wheels; but the whirr of them speaks most of his own eccentricities. Among the simple manufactures of the northern valleys were yarn hose, horn lanterns, and coarse druggets; but they have long ago been supplanted. Even among the poorest there is an inclination to turn their backs on honest homespun, and they now trick themselves out in webs of draggled embroidery. The old "stuffs" are gone, and materials with greater gloss and less substance are fast taking their place.

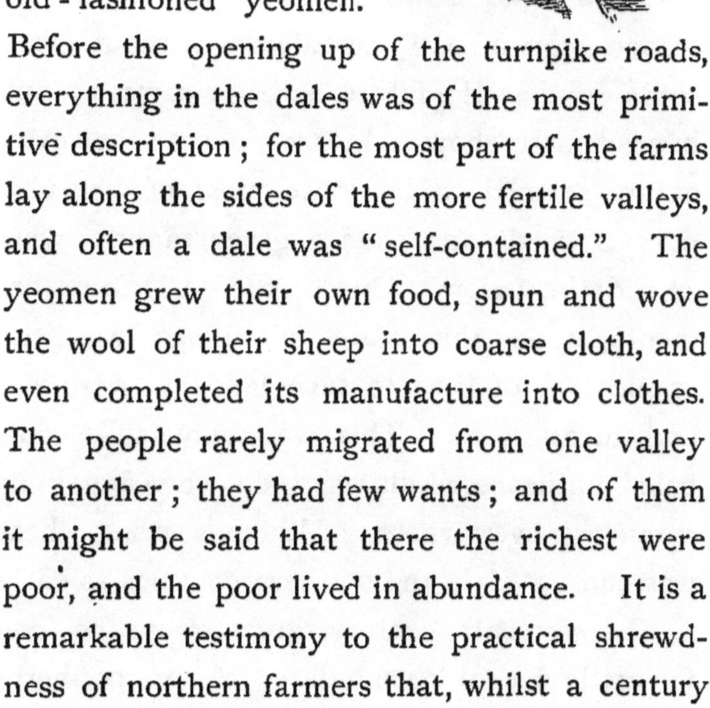

But to return to the old-fashioned yeomen. Before the opening up of the turnpike roads, everything in the dales was of the most primitive description; for the most part of the farms lay along the sides of the more fertile valleys, and often a dale was "self-contained." The yeomen grew their own food, spun and wove the wool of their sheep into coarse cloth, and even completed its manufacture into clothes. The people rarely migrated from one valley to another; they had few wants; and of them it might be said that there the richest were poor, and the poor lived in abundance. It is a remarkable testimony to the practical shrewdness of northern farmers that, whilst a century ago their farming was of the most primitive description, the depression in agriculture to-day is less felt among them than perhaps in any other part of the country.

Theirs was the "old system" of husbandry. When grass land was broken up it was sown with black oats, all the available manure of the little "estate" being bestowed upon it for the succeeding barley crop. The third year the land was laid down again to fallow with a second crop of oats, but always without grass seeds, so that the future herbage came no one knew exactly how. In such a case, however, nature seemed to let loose most of her ubiquitous weeds, and soon a green mantle overspread the fallow. One of the early improvements upon this state of things was the application of lime to such lands as were wet and moss-grown. This was universally ridiculed until the result was seen, when limekilns sprang up everywhere. Although spring wheat was cultivated in the northern counties as early as the sixteenth century, green crops as food for cattle are of recent date. As to pot-herbs and the produce of the vegetable garden generally, a century ago they were nearly unknown. Oat bread, dressed barley, and onions constituted the more cooling diet of the common people, with very little variety. By the middle of the eighteenth century, however, common-gardens were laid out in the environs of most north country towns, and at about the same time the culture of fruit trees became general. This was an important step; for not only did it supply a much-needed article of diet, but it was the beginning of a new industry. The more hardy fruit trees were peculiarly suited to the humid valleys of the north, and in time yielded enormous crops.

As yet the art of fattening cattle was but little understood, and the first experiments were tried on sheep in winter. This raised great hopes in the minds of breeders, for as yet the winter supply of animal food had proved wholly inadequate. The stock which was fed in autumn was killed off by Christmas, and with the exception of veal, scarcely any fresh meat appeared in the markets before the ensuing midsummer. This dearth the more substantial yeomen and manufacturers provided against by curing a quantity of beef at Martinmas, part of which was pickled in brine, the rest dried in the smoke of the capacious chimneys. On Sundays the farmers' wives boiled a huge piece of meat from the brine tub, which on that day was served hot. From that time as long as the joint lasted it came up cold, relish being given to it by the addition of oatmeal pudding. Hogs were slaughtered in great numbers between Christmas and Candlemas, the flesh being converted into bacon, which, with dried beef and mutton, afforded a change in spring. The only fresh provisions of winter consisted of eggs, poultry, geese, and ill-fed veal, the calves being then carried to market when two or three weeks old. In some of the northern rivers salmon was very abundant, and sold at twopence a pound.

I must now go on to speak of the dale dwellers. I need hardly say that at the beginning of the present century these belonged to the yeoman class, characteristic of the dales, but which is fast dying out. Looking round among our neighbours, I am almost startled to see how few yeomen remain—only a remnant of the original stock. At the period mentioned they almost wholly occupied the hill districts of the north, and what is more, they owned and farmed their holdings. They had all the virtues which attach to dwellers in a hill country. They tilled their grain patches, and the mountains were dotted with sheep. The farms were small, most of them ranging in value from £40 to £60 a year. Many of them had been held by one family for generations; I am sorry to say, however, that but too often as they descended from father to son they became heavily burdened with charges to the younger members. Mortgages and interest accumulated until the case of the statesman became hopeless and he was glad to find a purchaser for his little demesne. A series of bad seasons, loss of stock, or a prolonged winter would not unfrequently prove the last straw; or it sometimes happened that the yeoman's family became too large to be sustained by the estate. The natural result of this was that the small holdings were gradually merged into the larger ones, until now the process of assimilation may be said to be almost complete. The few that have survived have done so by consolidating small holdings where family interests were identical. In this way there are now numerous small farms worth one or two hundred pounds annually; whilst a very few more extensive ones bring in a rent of from £300 to £500. Some of the larger sheep farms now embrace whole valleys, and are from one to five thousand acres in extent. A number of small farms from £50 to £70 remain; but these are comparatively rare.

The old-fashioned statesman was essentially conservative. He lived along the sides of the dales, a mountain stream rushing through his rich meadows immediately below. His house and barns, built primarily with a view to shelter, were composed of rocks and boulders from the fell slopes, and were more like productions of nature than of art. The homesteads were generally planted at the base of the mountains, as there the soil is richest and deepest. The valley bottoms make productive meadows; and although the fell sheep often graze them far into summer, they yield abundant crops of grass in July. In these remote dales, however, the summer months are often wet ones, and the hay harvest is

sometimes very much delayed. Taking our stand by the margin of the valley stream we have, first, the meadow slip, then the "intack" or fell-side pasture, the grassing head, and, finally, the mountains. Many of the enclosed hill pastures are fringed with shaggy underwood and bosky dells, vestiges of the old forests. In the limestone caverns and recesses of the hills the remains of bears, wild boars, and wolves are found; while on one of the fells there still roams a herd of wild red deer. In most cases the statesman's holding was a sheep farm. He had right of "heaf" for 400 or 500 sheep upon the common. The times of lambing in spring, of washing in the fell dubs, and of shearing in late June, were among the events of the year. These sheep were of the hardy herdwick breed, climbing to the bleak fell tops at the coming of snow; and in this lay their safety. They were rarely buried in the drifts, and were clever at scratching away the snow to get at the hidden herbage.

At the time of which I speak the internal communication of the northern counties was bad indeed. The roads were so narrow that only pack horses could travel along them, and in this way the meagre traffic of the dales was conducted. Carriage roads there were none, and it was probably owing to this fact that, just as the yeomen spun their own wool, so they grew sufficient grain to last them through the year. Marks of the plough are often to be seen on the commons and moorlands; and in these marks may be read one reason of the rapid decline of the statesman class. About the beginning of the present century thousands of acres of the lower-lying commons were enclosed. The continental wars then raging had sent up all kinds of grain to a price unknown before. The yeoman reaped a rich harvest; fresh land was broken up, and some of it yielded enormously. Every available bit of land was ploughed, and corn crop after corn crop was taken off. These were flush times for the statesman, and lavish habits were contracted. Peace came, and brought with it its natural consequences.

The life of the fell folk must have been very lonely in winter. They rose and went to bed with the sun, their only artificial lights being made from rushes and mutton fat. Among the shippons in winter the candles were carried in old-fashioned horn lanterns, which were manufactured by themselves. There were no markets for their milk and butter, and so the former was converted into cheese, mostly of a very low quality.

CHAPTER VI.

I HAVE tried to set down a description of the lives of the "statesmen" who dwelt in the valley. And although the conditions of life might seem hard and everything primitive, yet it must be borne in mind that the class of fell folk next below that of the yeoman knew little of their comforts, and scarcely anything of their luxuries. At this period the labouring classes were badly housed; they subsisted chiefly on porridge of oatmeal, or dressed barley boiled in milk, with the addition of meal-bread, butter, and a very small quantity of salted meat. This diet told terribly upon the poorer population in spring; for ague set in with painful regularity. As the culture of esculent vegetables became more common, however, salted provisions fell into disrepute, and potatoes began to be generally though sparingly used. The cultivation of this root told healthily upon the inhabitants, and made them much better off than when they were wholly dependent upon grain. As the use and virtues of tea, then a foreign luxury, became better understood, neatly turned cups and saucers of wood made their appearance, these being commonly used instead of porcelain. The consumption of wheat became greater and more general after the introduction of tea, though at the beginning of the century wheat was never seen in the cottage of the northern labourer, and except on festal days but rarely made its appearance on the tables of the middle classes. Frugal housewives evinced their attachment to economy on these occasions by making their pastry of barley meal, which they veneered with a thin cake of flour. A curious custom survived until recently that shows the estimation in which wheaten bread was held by our ancestors. A small loaf was thought a fitting gift from the dead to the living, and every person who attended a funeral received one at the door of the deceased, and was expected to carry it home. The increased demand for wheat encouraged the hill farmers to pursue the modern methods of cultivating it; and though the experiment has everywhere since succeeded, thin cakes of oatmeal without leaven are yet daily eaten in quantities in almost all the houses of the mountain dales. It is upon this and oatmeal porridge that the famous wrestlers of the north are reared, and there seems but little likelihood of its disuse.

But perhaps the best idea of the early fell folk may be had by looking at their domestic life. And in this connection it must be said that their houses were ill-contrived and hardly in keeping with modern notions of decency. The water-supply was of course indispensable, but, instead of digging a well or conducting water to the houses, the homesteads were invariably built by the sides of the fell becks. Consequently, many of them stood in damp situations, and occasionally in autumn foaming torrents tore up the folds and washed away the outbuildings. These, like the houses, were low; a man of ordinary height could not pass the lintel without stooping. The floors were below the level of the ground without, and entrance was made by a descent of one or two steps. The basement was divided into three apartments; the "buttery," which constituted the general larder; the common hall, or kitchen, which formed the living room; and a slightly raised chamber, in which the master and mistress slept. The whole was either rudely paved with cobbles from the river bed or had a floor of flattened loam. There was no fire-grate, nor is there yet in many of the farmhouses of the mountain dales, and the peat or wood fire was laid on the hearth. The fires were "raked" at night, and some are known never to have been extinguished for half a century. "Raking" was easier than having to rekindle the fuel with the aid of a flint and steel, and was the universal practice. The chimney-place was one into which a cart might have been driven, being 12 feet or more in width, and open in front. In the funnel were hung joints of beef, mutton, and pork, while sometimes a dozen hams were smoking in the chimney. A long and sooty chain ending in a crook went up from the fire to a beam above, and this bore the heavy iron pans of the period. Many of these were supplied with a funnel by which to let the steam escape; and as there was nothing in the shape of ovens, all food was cooked by their aid. At every season of the

year streams of sooty water trickled down the wide chimneys; and the members of the household sat and went about their domestic duties with covered heads. In other instances the second storey of the house, called the loft, was open to the rafters, and constituted the sleeping apartment of the women and children.

In most cases there was but one chamber undivided by partitions ; and here the dependents were lodged—the men at one end, the women at the other, as already mentioned. Beyond a rope stretched across,—upon which coats and gowns, articles of both male and female attire, were hung promiscuously—there was no division whatever. In the houses of some of the statesmen of the provincial towns, where the custom was to provide lodging for journeymen as well as apprentices, matters were even worse.

The furniture of these northern homes was both rude in design and execution, but it was useful and homely, and eminently in keeping with the houses that contained it. The only quality they seem to have striven after in all their domestic utensils was serviceableness. Almost everything was of wood, pegs of the same substance invariably supplying the place of nails. Wooden latchets were fixed to doors and gates; indeed, iron was almost unknown in domestic architecture. One great feature of the country houses was their arks and chests. These were curiously and quaintly carved, with carvings "all made out of the carver's brain." Coleridge lived in a district where the work of the home-bred carver was everywhere to be seen, and

doubtless the above line in *Christabel* was so suggested. In the arks were kept oaten cake, malt, meal, preserves, and dried meats. These stores were largely drawn upon for bridal dowries. Old "china," pieces of dress material in flowered silk and satin, and a few pieces of plate—family heirlooms,—these found a place in the chest. The huge bedsteads in use were of massive oak, with testers of the same material. The chairs were generally made of clumsy wainscot, but some of them were fashioned from the trunks of hollow trees—the carpenter completing what time had begun. For table, there stood in the common hall a board of from three to five yards in length; this rustic board being furnished with forms or benches along its sides. Upon these the family and its guests were seated at meal times. Maple trenchers supplied the place of plates, and liquids of every description—milk, broth, beer,—were served in wooden vessels made with staves and hoops. Cold and wind, which freely found their way into the common hall by the chimney, as well as by the badly jointed doors and windows, were provided against by a screen placed in front of the turf fire. In the centre of the hearth stood a square upright staff, having a row of holes along one of its sides, and its lower end fixed in a log of wood. This simple contrivance supported the candlestick, which was thrust at a convenient height into one of the holes. In the warm though smoky retreat of the settle-nook, the family spent the long winter evenings in knitting, spinning flax, combing wool, and in other home industries. The conversation at such times, especially that of the elders, had one result, in perpetuating the credulity of the times. The talk constantly turned upon apparitions, omens, workers in witchcraft, and more innocent fairy tales. But at the beginning of a new era these things obtained less countenance, and a general change began. Provincial newspapers were started, and wonderfully enlarged the narrow world of country readers. Innovation came steadily from the south, and the rude artisans were ousted. Old handicrafts were subdivided; the cabinet maker invaded the province of the carpenter, the worker in metals that of the maker of wooden platters, and the great army of itinerants rapidly declined. The transformation during the period indicated exceeded that of any century that had preceded it in the history of the north.

In describing the lives and homes of the yeomen, I remarked that their sons and daughters went out to service. This spirit of honest independence contributed much to their success, and was one of their chief characteristics. And because it was so I am constrained to describe more at length the virtues of these hard-working sons and daughters, and to hold them up (at least in agricultural matters) for imitation and respect. The lives of this class, except by being bettered, have changed less than those of their superiors, and I shall endeavour to describe them as they exist pretty much to-day, not as they existed in times gone by. All our bread, all our wealth, comes from the land, and sometimes I am afraid we are apt to under-rate those who by their labour win it from the soil.

The farm labourer of the dales, then (and he

is more often than not the son of a small farmer or yeoman), is nothing akin to his southern brother. And it is probably no exaggeration to say that he is superior to him in every way in which comparison is possible. The southerner seems unable to lift himself above his surroundings, whilst the northerner almost invariably strives to do this, and not unfrequently succeeds. Much of this is probably owing to the fact that he is early sent to school, but at fourteen leaves home to earn his own living. He has been well schooled, in a way, and looks forward to "service." At the half-yearly hiring—Whitsuntide or Martinmas—after he has attained his "first majority," he goes to the nearest country town and stands in the market-place. He is attired in a brand new suit, with a capacious necktie of green and red. These articles he has donned upon the memorable morning, and as a gift from his parents they constitute his start in life. The country barber has left his head pretty much as the modern reaper leaves the stubble, and has not stinted him of grease for his money. As an outward and visible sign of his intention, the lad sticks a straw in his mouth and awaits the issue. For the first hour or so he keeps his eyes bent to the pavement, as though to read the riddle of his life there, but presently gains confidence to look about him. After waiting a greater part of the morning and seeing many of his fellow-men and maid-servants hired, he is accosted by a stalwart yeoman, who inquires if he wants a "spot"—a place, a situation. The lad replies that he does; that he is willing to do anything; and that he will engage for £4 the half-year—"if it pleases." A bargain is soon struck, and the stalwart urchin from the "fell-heads" marches off to lose himself in the giddy gaiety of the Fair. If ultimately he likes his "place," and is well and kindly treated, we may not see him again at hiring for a couple of years. During this time he has made himself generally useful, has become a good milker, and has shone conspicuously at hay and harvest. He has proved himself a "fine lad," and has had his wages raised by way of reward. At sixteen or seventeen he is stalwart enough to hire as a man, and now his wages are doubled; he asks and obtains £12 for the year, or even £14 if entering upon the summer half. The farm servants of the dales "live in," and have all found. They are well fed, well housed, and have their meals at the master's table. But if well fed they are hard worked, and in summer they often rise as early as three or four in the morning. In these parts, which constitute a vast grazing district, the labour of the farm servant is much more general and interesting than that of his southern brother, where the land is arable. Physically, the northern man is much the superior, and is generally an athlete. He is come of that stock which so stubbornly fought the Border wars, and now excels in wrestling, mountain racing, and following the wiry foxhounds among the hills. Of course these opportunities are only presented during the scant holidays in which he indulges, or in mid-winter, when there is little to be done beyond the tending of stock. It is necessary that the northerner should be a big sturdy fellow, since the ground which he has to work is rough, and he has not many helps in the way of machines to aid him. A few years ago, during the flourishing times of agriculture, the northern labourer obtained from £35 to £40 per annum, still, of course, "living in"; a few picked men could even command £45. Now, however, that we are come upon times of depression, the best men are glad to work for the first-named sum. In proportion, the girls are much better off in the matter of wages than the men. There is probably less competition among them, owing to the fact that there is a great temptation for country girls to migrate

and enter service in provincial towns. Here they are not so hard worked as in the farm-houses, and have the satisfaction of being engaged in what they esteem a much more "genteel" occupation.

Many of the men, when about thirty years of age, are able to take small farms of their own. Nearly all the statesmen's sons do this, and probably without any outside help; for, as a class, these labourers are not only industrious but thrifty. I knew a man who had saved £120, which sum he had divided and deposited in three banks. This was his whole wealth, and he told me he did not want to lose his hard-earned savings if the banks should "break." His object was to acquire a small farm, and he has now succeeded.

From the fact of "living in," as nearly all the valley servants do, it need hardly be said that early marriages are rare. All the better men look forward to the time when they can have a farm of their own; and when they obtain a holding, they then look out for a wife. This fact alone speaks well for their thrift; but it has its dark side. How far the two things are connected may be a matter of speculation; but it is notorious that the number of illegitimate children in the north is far above the average, and most of these undoubtedly are born of the agricultural classes. The registers of the country churches abundantly prove this. Still, it is pleasing to be able to record the fact that in the dales, sooner or later, those who have been wronged "are made honest women of" by marriage.

In the remoter dales the most primitive manners and customs still prevail, and the farm servants are as conservative as their masters. Not only are they so in politics, but in their agricultural implements and their whole surroundings. At one time of the year the "sledding" of the peat constitutes a considerable portion of the work. Nothing but sticks and turf are used as fuel; and the peat has to be first graved, then stacked, and finally brought from the moorlands on sledges. This is done in autumn. Spring is occupied in tending the mountain sheep, the time of lambing being a particularly busy one. Sheep washing is a busy time, and shearing, a month later, brings quite an annual festival. The "clipping," where the holdings are sheep farms, is one of the great events of the year. Before the days of "clipping," "salving" the sheep came in late autumn, and brought a time of terribly hard work. The process was slow, and sometimes a thousand sheep had to be got through. To enable them to do this the men had candles fixed in their caps, and worked both early and late. Now salving is superseded, and a thing of the past. Half the time of the northern farm labourer of the hill districts is taken up in connection with the sheep.

Whenever northern farmers go south they endeavour to graze more and plough less land, and so follow the lines in which they have been reared; and it is generally admitted that they are successful. Just now many of them are obtaining southern farms which have almost gone out of cultivation, and some of them have already shown what can be done in this way. They pay but little rent, and will doubtless do well with their bargains. In short, the northern farm labourer, wherever he appears, drives his brothers out of the field, and has already left his mark upon southern grass lands.

CHAPTER VII.

THE education of the people of the dales has always been of a fairly high standard. This is probably owing to the prevalence of good grammar schools in the neighbourhood. It is doubtless to these schools that we owe a host of worthies who have sprung from the hill districts, — men who have made names for themselves, and who have been a power in the land. I might mention many such, four or five of whom have sprung from our own dale. The men who were at the head of these schools had each received a good classical education, and also knew something of the mathematics. Free schools were in almost every parish, and this in addition to the parochial school, which usually stood near the church. These latter were endowed with a stipend for the maintenance of a master, who instructed children however poor, if only they chose to attend, in English, Latin, and Greek. The nature of the establishment entitled the preceptor to nothing more than his salary; but the parents of his pupils thought proper to reward his diligence by an annual gratuity at Shrovetide, called a cock-penny to this present day. John Dalton has recorded how a singular donation was made to Wreay school by a Mr Graham, gentleman, about which it may be interesting to inquire. This donation consisted of a silver bell, weighing two ounces, upon which was engraved "Wreay Chapple, 1655, to be fought for annually on Shrove Tuesday by cocks." About three weeks previous to that day the boys fixed upon two of their school-fellows for captains, whose parents were able and willing to bear the expense of the approaching contest; and the master, on entering school, was saluted by the boys throwing up their caps, and the exclamation "Dux, dux!" On Shrove Tuesday the two captains, attended by their friends and school-fellows, who were distinguished by blue and red ribbons, marched in procession from their various homes to the village green, where each produced three cocks, and the bell was appended to the hat of the victor, in which manner it was handed down from one successful captain to another. In 1836 the cock-fighting at Wreay was suppressed by the Rev. R. Jackson, and in its place there is now an annual hunt. The noted bell of 1655, a parochial institution for 217 years, was stolen a few years ago from the house where the convivial meetings used to be held, and where it had so often graced the hats of "cocking champions," or the white rods of sham mayors. This custom was continued at most of the dale schools until a very late period, and was presided over by the schoolmaster. Many of the famous cockpits even now exist, but they are grass-grown and unused. It may be added that in many of the endowed schools as much as half the master's salary had, by arrangement of the founders, been made to depend on the cock-pennies. With regard to the actual fighting, the plucky birds were supposed to set an excellent example to the virtuous youths, and to stir them to noble emulation in fighting the Gallic or any other wide-throated cock that dared to crow defiance and flap his wings. This barbarous sport and others have passed away before the diffusion of knowledge and feeling, and the higher intellectual and moral culture of the people. It may be questioned, however, whether the step of substituting the hare for the pitting of two gamecocks against each other tends to prove a higher degree of civilisation. But, be this as it may, hunting in the hills is enjoyed by rich and poor alike, and is the chief out-door winter pastime of the statesmen and yeomanry. And Mr Wordsworth has asserted, when speaking of the independent spirit of the dalesmen, that when the hounds were out "not a soul in the village" would remain for want of leisure to enjoy the sport. It is said that the plan of tuition here described answered two purposes of unequal importance, for it handed down the favourite diversions of the country from father to son, and furnished every hamlet with its scholar, who was prepared on all occasions to contend for the palm of erudition with the learned of other townships and distant parishes. True it is that many men who were really famous sprang from these mountain dales—a cardinal, an archbishop, a half-dozen bishops, eminent travellers, and a general, as well as several scientists and men of letters.

The above has reference to the higher of the two classes of schools which existed at one time. The parochial and village schools almost confined their attention to the teaching of writing, reading, and "the science of arithmetic." Contemporary with these schools, however, were a number of travelling tutors—itinerant scriveners or writing-masters—who went on circuit and had regular customers. These men had a strict sense of honour in keeping to their own ground, and in their search for pupils they were frequently hired into gentlemen's families for weekly wages. It is said that many of them were ingenious men, and were generally welcome at the "great" houses of their patrons; but as education came to be looked upon more seriously, the occupation fell gradually into disrepute. One change in the two systems of education which the advancing progress of the times brought with them was, among others, a peculiar one. Classical scholars were no longer to be found among the husbandmen; for all that received any education were put to agriculture or trade, with the exception of the few that were intended for one or other of the learned professions. The good sense of latter-day country education appears in few instances more conspicuously than in the attention that is now paid to female education. It was formerly thought necessary to teach a girl the art of reading, that she might peruse the Bible for herself. The daughters of better families also learned to scrawl a hand which was not always very legible; but the advantages of arithmetic were reserved for the boys. This practice created a great disparity of intellect in the two sexes; for it was not an uncommon thing in former days to find an illiterate woman married to a yeoman who could read the Testament in Greek, and who was acquainted with the best writers of the Augustan age.

In a previous chapter it was remarked that the oldest inhabitants of the valley talked to the day of their death of the first chaise which had invaded it. I have also said that the dale was gorge-like—there was a way into it, but none out. So embosomed was it among the mountains, so hemmed in, that to strangers its entrance might have proved a puzzle. The valley is about five miles in length, and just as you emerge from it a fine turnpike road presents itself—a road passing over the fells, it is true, but once used by the Romans—made by them perhaps—and constituting, at the time of which I write, the well-used coach road; so that if there was but little travelling in the dale, there were plenty of travellers to be seen passing at the foot of it. Children were promised that "sometime" they should go to "Dale End," and many of them looked forward to this for years. Speaking generally of the hill district, wheel carriages were very little used for private intercourse or trade. Persons of both sexes made short journeys on horseback, women being commonly seated on pillons behind the men. Very few people made long excursions from home, except the manufacturers of the small contiguous country towns, and many of these travelled on foot in quest of

orders for their worsted stockings and linsey woolsey. Carriers did not employ waggons, but drove gangs of pack-horses, each of which was preceded by a bell-horse, and the owners reckoned a woman equivalent to half a pack in lading their beasts of burden. The predi-

lection for transporting all kinds of commodities on horseback was so general that even the fuel consumed in the small country towns was conveyed in this manner. Greytown lies to the south of our valley, and so important were its principal manufactures, that two hundred and ninety-four pack-horses entered and left the town with merchandise. Although I have spoken of a "turnpike," along which these trains of men and horses went, the road proper has only been made in comparatively recent times,—before the horses had merely followed ill-defined tracks. Waggons had not as yet come in, and the few coals which were burned at the great houses were conveyed in sacks on the backs of galloways. For convey ing turf and peats from the mosses "halts" were used. These were a pair of strong wicker hampers, joined by a pack saddle, and hung across a horse's back; they were put to various uses in husbandry—to those offices which are now performed by carts. Of course the use of coal in outlying districts is of comparatively recent date, as no mention is made of it in accounts of household expenses of early times. Before peats were cut from the mosses wood was the principal *fire-elden.* The next progression in travelling was the substitution of carts for halts. But these were ill-contrived, the wheels consisting of two circular boards immovably fixed, without spokes, to the ends of a cylindrical axle. This arrangement required the axle itself to revolve beneath the cart, where it was kept in place by two pairs of parallel wooden pins that projected downwards from the frame bottom. But with the opening up of the turnpike roads an epoch in the travelling of the country came about, and I have already mentioned the commencement of the coaching times, and the effect which these had upon the dalesfolk.

CHAPTER VIII.

MY father had two hobbies, to which he was about equally attached. He was a great entomologist in his way, and wrote tracts on "Temperance." So far as I know, he was the first and only one of our family that had advocated total abstinence from fermented liquor. It was certainly not because he was morally weak that he adopted this principle, but rather to set a good example to his parishioners. Intemperance was not one of the prominent weaknesses of the dale, but it must be confessed that one or two of the yeomen came home tipsy as certainly as they visited Greytown on market day. As to the entomology, there was always abundant proof of this at home. In summer and autumn rare moths and butterflies were pinned to the dining-room curtains in very great abundance, to our infinite delight and our poor mother's slight irritation. My father, I believe, added two or three insects to the then known British species, one of which was new to science. This was called after our name by one of the great scientists, and we all felt very proud at what we thought the distinction conferred upon us. I am bound to say, however, that I have never yet seen the name in print, nor have my brothers, although we have often tried to find it. One of our red-letter days was when a copy of the *Transactions* of a learned society arrived at our home, and contained a list of the insects of our valley, written by my father. We all of us were very proud, as in assisting him we felt that part of the distinction belonged to us. We read the learned paper with its hard names many times over, and especially a little postcript attached to it by the editor of the *Review*. This learned man remarked that the list was an exceedingly complete one; that it was evidently from a district rich in insect life; finally he held it up for imitation, urging upon others to do conscientiously for their districts what my father had done for ours, and concluded by pointing out that in this way the cause of science could best be served. There was only one thing to damp our pleasure, which was, that, instead of appending his name, my father had merely written his initials. As I have said, we were disappointed, and told my father that the list, so far as the signature went, might have been compiled by anyone, and that he had robbed himself of half the honour. He answered that in what he had written he had endeavoured to add his mite to science, and in this he had his reward. And so we were silenced. Loving natural history as he did, my father encouraged each of us to take up some branch of it. He impressed upon us, too, the necessity of close and accurate observation, and said that, if we were to excel our fellows, we ought each to have a specialty, and pursue it with a great ardour.

I do not think the farmers set much store by our studies in natural history; and I believe some of them held us in rather slight contempt for pursuing them. What practical good could come of it? Was it going to bring us our bread? And because our neighbours could not find answers within themselves to these self-imposed questions, our pet projects were both mercilessly reviewed and summarily condemned. We were illustrative of types of mental weakness out of which no good things could be expected to come. In after years I knew exactly what they thought of us, for I found their very ideas incorporated in *The Ingoldsby Legends*. And when I read them, I saw our own pictures start up vividly before me.

> Still poking his nose into this thing or that,
> At a gnat, or a bat, or a rat, or a cat,
> Or great ugly things, all legs and wings,
> With nasty long tails armed with nasty long stings.

Or take this other description of the popular verdict against us, for it is even more succinct:

> He would pore by the hour o'er a weed or a flower,
> Or the slugs which came crawling out after a shower;
> Black beetles and bumble bees, bluebottle flies,
> And moths were of no small account in his eyes;
> An industrious flea he'd by no means despise;
> While an old daddy longlegs, whose long legs and thighs
> Passed the common in shape, or in colour, or size,
> He was wont to consider an absolute prize.

But this scant justice which our early studies obtained did us little harm. My father was always ready to lend us his ready sympathy and knowledge, and my dear mother expressed herself pleased that we seemed to have such a fondness for nature. Nothing but good could come of it, she thought; and I well remember her saying she could not understand how anyone with a deep love of the works of the Creator in his heart could ever become quite depraved. The members of our family, however, were not the only naturalists that the valley had produced. So rich was it in natural objects, that I am fully convinced most of the yeomen were naturalists themselves without knowing it. Although they never set anything down on paper, they were keen observers, and I have heard them describe in the most interesting way the various traits of the live creatures they met. But two or three had been born in the dale, at long intervals, who had afterwards distinguished themselves in science. One of these was John Wilson. Wilson was born and lived in the dale, and we were very proud to think that he wrote the first great work on English botany. This worthy man came upon the scene when botany, in its best sense, had made but little progress. He was one of those naturalists who did much to place the science on the broad scientific basis upon which it now rests. His predecessors had mostly comprehended the subject as it taught them of the herbs and simples of the wood.

Rue, cinque-foil, gill, vervain, and agrimony
Blue-vetch and trilium, hawk-weed, sassafras,
Milkweeds and murky brakes, quaint pipes and sundew.

Like his predecessors he clung fondly to the old English names, and loved to wrap about the flowers the attributes his fathers had done. This knowledge of "herbalism" had been profound, but he would have none of it. Wilson was a truly remarkable man; and although there is all that intenseness and simplicity anent his dealings with nature that there had been in connection with the old workers who preceded him, yet his work is of an eminently scientific character. They were not always infallible observers, and frequently tripped in their facts. Wilson rarely did so.

He found botany as a science a veritable maze, all without a plan; but at his death he left it somewhat systematised. I have said that Wilson was born in our valley, and may add that he came of pious yeomen folk, who were poor enough, except in the possession of many stern virtues. The primitive dale must have proved a very paradise to him, as it was so secluded, and certainly had never been invaded by science prior to his coming. This pleasant environment did not last long. In the fulness of his boyish enthusiasm he roamed over the hills like a partridge. The very isolation referred to, which was a merit in one way, rendered the people a prey to the grossest superstition. Our botanist made long, lonely journeys, often at night, among the hills and woods, and by the sea. The fell folk said that the nightly calling which took him so far afield might be honest; but they shook their heads, and some even ventured to say that he was a "wise man"—a dealer in mysteries, and given to dark sayings. It was probably this evil repute which gathered around him, and the want of books, that caused him to leave the dale and go to a small market town about ten miles off. And, maybe, this enforced migration was well. He had studied long and hard in his native valley, and there had had abundant and rare material. At home he had only an old "Herbal," which he well knew was as full of inaccuracies as superstition. Now he had good guides, and found himself within reach of the best books on the subject, and came into connection with those who had like interests to himself. Some of these were really remarkable workers—workers who stood out far above the common run of men. They put before Wilson the then standard works of his own pet subject, and of the contents of these, with his already acquired knowledge and native understanding, he quickly made himself master. But none of the works to which he had access were so good as the one he was himself destined to write. They were styled "scientific"; but the first law of science is order, and, as yet, there was only chaos. Our botanist was the great mind born to perceive and exhibit such order from the then ascertained elements of botany so far as collected. I need only further say that Wilson laboured hard for many years, working at his book the while he pursued his trade. When it was published it came out in English, and not in Latin. The author had set out with a well-defined plan, and executed it in an admirable manner. It was a strong and original work, a very monument of accurate observation and the genius of hard work. The botanist's early wanderings among the fells were stamped upon every page, and Wilson was wont to say that he never could have succeeded without that early life which he loved so well. And so one of our worthies produced his *Synopsis of British Plants.*

I have already said something of our studies in natural history, and also of the desire which my father had that we should each take up some specialty instead of working indiscriminately. He knew from experience how many a keen intellect had rusted, shut out as it was among the isolation of the hills. If ever that fate should be ours, as it had been his, he felt that, by encouraging us in some scientific study, he had done what he could to guard against the breeding of *ennui*, and that science, whichever branch we might take up, would teach us the habits of close and accurate observation. My father knew little of birds, but in his diary he kept records of the arrival and departure of the rarer summer visitants; and, speaking for myself, it was these entries, and the observations which they suggested, that first interested me in ornithology. From that time I have always taken an intense interest in birds. I propose to set down here a very short account of those that visited our valley, and I must also sketch one or two of its main physical characteristics. These are essential to the better understanding of the subject. It is hemmed in on three sides, and on the south sweeps away and loses itself in the undulations of a wooded plain. An arm of the sea touches upon the confines of the plain, and thus it will be seen that the district includes tracts of a very diversified nature. It is probable that this makes the woods, and streams, and meadows of the valley so rich in bird life, and the fact of the quietude of the spot being rarely broken.

Owing to the close proximity of the hills, the Raptores have always been the most prominent birds of the valley. They are not so common now as formerly, though the sparrow-hawk may still be seen in the woodlands, and the kestrel holds its own among the rocks of the scaurs. The beautiful circling kites have left Gled Hill, and the merlin falcon has flown, never more to return. Occasionally an osprey visits the still mountain tarns on migration, and ravens cross from moor to moor, uttering their dismal "Croak, croak, croak!" The old dismantled

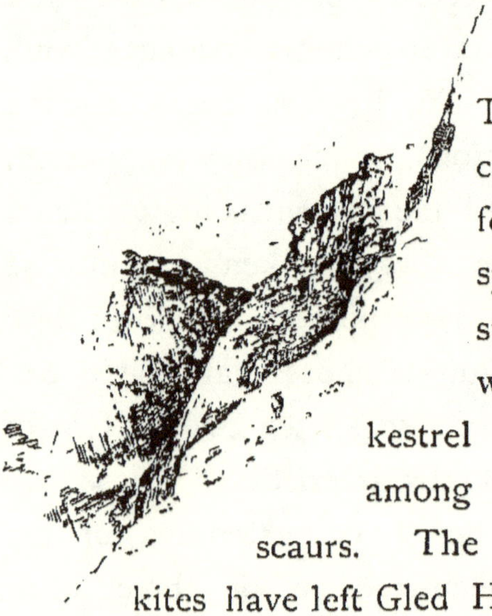

Hall has its pair of screech-owls, and the tawny owl makes night mournful by her hooting in the stiller woods. The more rare long-eared and short-eared owls are occasionally found on the lower-lying mosses which skirt the waters of the brackish creek. The great grey shrike, or butcher-bird, visits the copses which are likely to provide food for its larder, and I have found the red-backed species among the hedges which encircle the moat of an old lichened ruin. The spotted and pied fly-catchers come to us as our first summer visitants, the former being much more common than the latter. They establish themselves everywhere along the trout streams, obtaining food from the insects of the overhanging boughs. The pretty white-breasted dipper, or water-crow, haunts our rocky stream, and early builds its nest along the Greenwash tributaries. Companion of the ouzel is the brightly-plumaged kingfisher, with its metallic tints. You hear its whistle far down stream; it comes through the old ivied bridge, darts past, and is gone — gone to the dripping moss by the waterfall, where the female halcyon is hatching her eggs. The song-thrush is everywhere, and often in spring several may be heard at once, filling the whole glade with their warblings. Of the other thrushes, the "orange-billed merle" floods the copse with its mellow song on summer evenings. The blackbird stays about our hedgerows the whole of the year, as does the missel-thrush; while the fieldfare and the redwing come to our holly-berries in winter from the pine wastes of Norway. The ring-ouzel still holds its own among the fell becks, and there trills out its weird and not unmusical song. The hedge accentor, the redbreast, and the redstart are common, the last coming to us in April to rear its young. It is quite the most beautiful of the warblers, and its brilliant plumage shows well against the sombre hues of the limestone.

It is now that so many other of the *Sylviadæ* come—the soft-billed warblers of the wood-bird kind. Among these are the stonechat, whinchat, and wheatear. The first, a shy bird of the common, builds its nest among the gorse; the second in like situations, or among broom or juniper bushes; while the wheatear lays its pale blue eggs in some old crannied wall. Then come the willow, wood, and garden warblers—the white-throat, the sedge-bird, and the blackcap. The sedge and willow warblers have their nests among the aquatic plants of the tarns and meres, and their game preserves in the stalks and leaves of the swaying grasses. Sweetest of wood-birds are the warblers, and sweetest songster of the choir the blackcap warbler. This bird is sometimes called the "mock nightingale," and we have known persons listening, as they believed, to Philomela when the blackcap was the only bird under the night. The nightingale has never extended its northern haunt to our valley, although it is difficult to ascertain why this should be so. The whole of the warblers and white-throats may be found in our more sheltered woods, where they breed after the first weeks of May. The old Honeybee Woods are the chief haunt of these delicate songsters.

Owing to the number of larch and fir plantations which border the slopes of our valley, the family of tits has always been well represented. The first of these is the golden-crested regulus, the smallest of British birds, though by no means the rarest. The crested wren, the great, blue, cole, marsh, and long-tailed tits are all of them common. This miniature family of acrobats disperse themselves over their breeding haunts in summer, nesting for the most part in holes in trees, but in winter scour the woods in companies in search of food. Often they may be seen, hanging head downwards, abstracting the seeds from the hardened cones. Flocks of Bohemian waxwings are sometimes shot during the severity of winter, and occasionally chattering crossbills appear among the pines at the same season. The pied and grey wagtails stay with us throughout the year; while a third species comes to our creeks in April, and thence proceeds inland. The meadow and tree pipits we have, the latter in autumn leaving the vicinities of farmsteads, where it breeds, for warmer climes. In summer the skylark is everywhere common, and the sweet-singing woodlark rare. The snowflake, or mountain bunting, is a little northern visitor which comes to our fell slopes in winter. The common and yellow buntings have their nests among the tangled herbage of the roadside, and the black-headed bunting, or reed-sparrow, is everywhere common in the vicinity of water. Owing to the better cultivation of the valley "intacks" the goldfinch has become almost extinct. The bullfinch, the greenfinch, and the chaffinch are common everywhere, and more than half the bird-sounds one hears in summer are due to the last named. The beautiful mountain finch, or brambling, is rare. Linnets and siskins go through life together, ranging the fields in search of cress and wild mustard seed. In summer they are among the broom, in winter among the fallows. At the same season we frequently find the lesser redpole among the nut-tree tops, though its relative, the twite, keeps to higher ground. The peregrine and the carrion-crow are much more rare than formerly, as is also the hooded crow; their haunts, too, are getting farther and farther away. Rooks, jackdaws, and magpies are everywhere on the increase, though this can hardly be said of the jay and the wryneck. The garrulous blue jay is confined to a few oak copses, and the wryneck to one belt of wood. The little mouse-like creeper and the wren have protection in their diminutiveness, and consequently abound. The hoopoe is also an occasional visitant, and has been more than once taken. The lap of May brings that wandering voice, the cuckoo, which has been preceded, a few days, by the sweet birds of return—the swallows, martins, and swifts. The night-jar, or goatsucker, follows a few days later, and flies immediately to the coppice woods, preferring those where huge slabs of limestone pave the ground, as on these the birds love to bask, and between their crevices they lay their eggs. The ringdove and the rock-dove haunt the woods, though the turtledove comes but rarely. The semi-domestic pheasant flourishes only under protection, though the more hardy partridge has her oak-leaf nest under the glowing gorse bushes in every congenial situation. The indigenous red grouse is common on the moors, the blackcock rare. Occasionally the timid quail rears her brood amid the long summer grass. The bittern has ceased to boom in the bog, but the gaunt heron still pursues his solitary trade. The beautiful golden plover stays with us on its way to the more northern hills; and the common green plover, peewit, or lapwing, breeds everywhere over the fallows. The curlew still gives out its weird whistle on the fells, and hovers around the farm lights on stormy nights. The rare ruff and the green sandpiper occasionally come to the mosses by the Greenwash; and here in winter may be heard the wild clangour and cries of innumerable sea birds.

CHAPTER IX.

CLOSELY connected with the valley, either by ties of friendship or by reason of its natural productions, were two remarkable men, of whom I should like to speak. These were John Gough and John Dalton. The first was born just outside the dale, the other in a more distant valley among the Cumbrian hills. Both visited at our family house, and I have heard many interesting reminiscences in connection with these visits. Dalton's early career was commenced at Greytown, where Gough was born, and the two were bound to the valley in many ways. Dalton was pupil to Gough. It may be well to speak of the latter first.

Gough was closely connected with Manchester, with its learned societies, and many of its famous sons. By Dr Kitto and other writers he was generally styled the "blind philosopher." Dalton was president of the

Manchester Philosophical Society, and no fewer than fourteen papers, mostly on experimental philosophy and natural history, were read by Gough before the society, of which his former pupil was president. Wordsworth was a personal friend, and speaks of him in the following lines :—

Methinks I see him—how his eyeballs rolled
Beneath his ample brow, in darkness paired ;
But each instinct with spirit, and the frame
Of the whole countenance alive with thought,
Fancy, and understanding ; while the voice
Discoursed of natural and moral truth
With eloquence, and such authentic power,
That in his presence humbler knowledge stood
Abashed, and tender pity overawed.

Gough became blind when a little over two years of age, so that his knowledge of outward objects must have been exceedingly limited. Having stated this fact, I should like to say something of his studies in practical natural history, and to indicate the manner in which this knowledge was acquired. It was related by him in after life, as an instance of his retentive memory, that he could minutely describe the form and contortions of an earth-worm shown him by his father as it crawled over a flower-bed in the garden. Gough was come of the old Quaker stock of the north country, his father being Thomas Gough, a skinner and glover of Wyresdale, in Lancashire. His mother was the daughter of a well-to-do yeoman, who owned a valuable estate on the banks of Windermere. Our future philosopher was born in 1757, and the first few years of his life must have been dark indeed. But it may be readily understood that the senior Gough, a devoted and pious Friend of the old school, did everything in his power to make the time pass less heavily with the blind lad. In a simple, homely way his education was now commenced. It consisted at first in submitting to his touch every object that might be safely handled, and in this way he gained some idea of external form and other qualities. But brighter days were at hand. In the spring and summer he was led abroad in the fields, and about this time a flood of light rushed upon him. Nature, by that wonderful law of compensation, quickened to a marvellous degree the senses which were left to him. As he sat among the grass and flowers the sunlight glinted down upon him, the warm wind brought on its breath the sweet smell of flowers, and it seemed as if to him the birds sang, and the squirrels chattered. At this time he would examine, in his own simple way, such specimens as his guide brought to his hands. His first actual lesson in botany seems to have been given by an old weaver, at whose house he was wont to visit. He was attracted to a window by the sweet smell of flowers, and groping his way thither he examined some plants contained in pots. The differences he found, and which his fine sense of touch enabled him to detect, showed at once that here was a wide field for investigation. From this time botany became one of his favourite pursuits. And now it was that a curious coincidence occurred, which served to confirm an early impression. He was lying upon a bank whilst his father angled, when the latter submitted to him a worm. With a cry of delight he immediately recognised in the soft-bodied creature the likeness in form to the one he had seen in the garden. This incident, slight as it may appear, gave a further impetus to his studies, and from this time he became deeply interested in zoology. And now he was lifted from darkness, his ways henceforth were ways of light, for nature seemed to have taken him to her broader bosom. Domestic animals he knew, as it were, by heart, but was surprised beyond measure to learn that there were thousands of others which roamed in a state of nature. Gough listened with rapt attention to the popular descriptions of these creatures read to him by his father, and when the announcement was made that a large travelling menagerie was about to visit Greytown, his manifestations of delight were almost beyond control. Previous to its coming he neither ate nor slept, and when it actually arrived he entered the cages of the quieter animals, examining each in turn, passing his fingers over them, his face beaming the while. Of the larger carnivora, however, he knew nothing, beyond hearing their low mutterings and growls, or the thuds as they bounded about the cages. He went home interested, but disappointed. Once there nothing could restrain him; he urged, he petitioned, he pleaded, and he had his way. Father and son returned to the menagerie, and his case was laid before the proprietor. The extreme danger was pointed out; but the lad pleaded his own cause and triumphed—he was to examine the lions, tigers, and leopards, even the polar bears. He entered every cage save that of the hyenas, and, as may be supposed, the time so spent was never forgotten.

Shortly after this, when Gough was about six years of age, he was sent to the Friends' school at Greytown, of which a Mr Bewley was then master—a man whose mind was not only stored with a vast amount of classical and scientific knowledge, but one who was passionately fond of natural history. "Like master like scholar," and from this time

Gough's life was shaped. At school he was taught Latin, with which he made rapid progress; but the study of plant life he loved best, and about this time we find him writing as follows: "My progress in botany proved very slow for a long time. It is true I never desisted from the pursuit, for every plant that fell in my way became an object of careful scrutiny. I treasured up in memory the forms of a multitude of vegetables, so as to afterwards recognise many of them, when I came to read their descriptions."

In his thirteenth year Gough was informed by his father that two Greytown men had written of plants, at which the young naturalist expressed surprise, not knowing that botany had been treated of in books. He set to work, however, and by hard reading and examining specimens soon made himself master of John Wilson's *Synopsis of British Plants* and Hudson's *Flora Anglica.* He then studied more advanced works, formed a botanical class among his schoolfellows, and made an herbarium. Hudson followed the old method of

Linnæus, and this was the one best adapted to Gough. The classification depended much upon the number of stamens in a flower, which Gough easily determined by inserting the tip of his tongue between the petals. His delicate fingers ran with lightning-like rapidity over the specimens brought to be named from far and near, and if the flower or plant happened to be a rare one, his face beamed as he told its name, its natural order, and not unfrequently added a scrap of interesting folk-lore. And he was rarely mistaken; he pronounced quickly, and skilful botanists never questioned his verdict. Indeed, Dr Withering, with whom he was in frequent correspondence, "informed his blind contributor that he would accept his habitats and remarks without reserve, and without any more specimens for verification." Gough was loved by all about him, and though many friends tried good-naturedly to puzzle him, none ever succeeded. A plant once seen, or rather felt, he never forgot; and though the flower submitted to him might have its home among the Alps or in the Tropics, so well acquainted was he with our own flora that he invariably referred it by analogy to its right natural order. Strange as it may seem, the colours of flowers he could determine by touch ; and on this subject we find him, in after years, writing a scientific essay. Gough and Wordsworth were intimately acquainted, and throughout the works of the latter frequent allusions are made to his blind friend. It happened once that the bard of Rydal and Coleridge were walking among the mountains, when the conversation turned upon Gough. They were approaching Grisedale Tarn, when one of them plucked a bit of *Silene acaulis* (Moss campion), which, being rare, it was proposed should be submitted to Gough, with the avowed object of puzzling him. It was sent, and when put into his hand, he said, "I have never examined this plant before, but it is *Silene acaulis.*" The fact is, that the blind philosopher had heard read some beautiful elegiac verses written by Wordsworth upon his brother John, in which this little mountain flower was vividly described. The description had so lived upon him that he immediately recognised it after a lapse of twelve years. Another trick devised to deceive Gough is worth recording. If rarer flowers failed to puzzle him, he might be deceived by abnormal specimens of commoner ones. Accordingly a plant was put into his hands which had been contorted and twisted. His fingers and tongue were quickly brought into requisition as he ran over the parts of the flower. A quiet smile of triumph played over his features as he quietly remarked, "I'm puzzled now, unless this be a potato flower." Gough was right, and his questioner turned away abashed.

Although, as I have said, John Dalton was born among the Cumbrian hills, yet upon his removal to Greytown he became a pretty frequent visitor to one or two houses in the valley. Like Gough he was a Quaker, and it may have been through the former that he came to know some of the families in the dale. This was in his young days, whilst he was still a schoolmaster, and before he removed to

Manchester. From these isolated visits sprang a deep love of our valley, and an acquaintance with many of its treasures. It was here that Dalton collected various natural history specimens, and also conducted a number of his earliest meteorological experiments. He had come from his quiet Cumbrian home to join his cousin, George Bewley (together with Jonathan, his brother, as assistant), in teaching the Quaker school at Greytown. What we hear nowadays about Dalton is all as a great chemist —as the author of the Atomic Theory. Therefore, to mention the way in which the young philosopher came to the scene of his first labours may not be uninteresting. He started from his humble thatched home with an exceedingly tiny bundle of personal comforts. These he supplemented on the way by an umbrella—a piece of extravagance, it has been urged, for such a poor philosopher. The distance from Eaglesfield to Greytown was forty-four miles, and the road lay through the heart of the beautiful Lake country. The long journey was accomplished in a single day, and when Dalton reached his destination he found it a grey, old-fashioned town of about 10,000 inhabitants. These same inhabitants had always been somewhat in advance of the times in the matter of book learning and general culture, and hence knew the value of a good education. The straggling borough, with its ancient charter and many rights, based its broad foundations upon Quakerism. Most of its leading people were Friends, and as the members of this quiet sect were mostly engaged in trades which they themselves had built up, the little place was quite one of manufacturing activity. Woollens constituted the staple trade, and by their motto on the town shield the people asserted that wool was their bread. Although, as I have said, there were but 10,000 people in the place, the Friends' meeting-house provided for 1200 of them. This was a large, plain building, eminently satisfactory as to its foundations, and withal fairly comfortable. If it was not always filled at the ordinary meeting for worship, it was filled to overflowing on "Quarterly Meeting" days. Upon these occasions Friends came in from all the outlying country meetings—from the dales and the fell-heads—and created quite a quiet kind of excitement in the town. They wore their quaint attire in sombre brown, or grey, or drab, or fawn, the wealthier women Friends in soft silks or satin, the yeomen's wives in more sober homespun. Just across the way from the meeting-house was the school in which the children of its members were taught, and it

was to this that Dalton came as teacher. In 1785 his cousin, George Bewley, the then head-master, retired, and the brothers Dalton announced their intention of continuing the school, "where youths will be carefully instructed in English, Latin, Greek, and French; also writing, arithmetic, merchants' accounts, and the mathematics." Whether boarders had previously resided in the school I do not know, but now the brothers offered to take these on reasonable terms, and their sister Mary came from Eaglesfield to act as housekeeper. The young Daltons had an amazing capacity for hard work. They increased their income by "drawing conditions," collecting rents, making wills, and by constituting themselves notaries public. During the period of this struggle Joseph and Deborah Dalton visited their children in Greytown, and brought with them cakes, cloth, and other home produce. Upon these occasions they tramped the forty-four miles on foot, caring for no personal fatigue, so long as their children's wants were supplied. In the following year to which this refers the brothers issued a second circular, which comprehended a curriculum of the very widest description. This somewhat remarkable document embraced everything that was taught in the highest schools, together with every subject that could be comprehended under the head of Natural

Philosophy, and there was a postscript to the effect that the brothers would give private instruction in the use of the globes after school

hours; that they could conveniently teach a considerable number of scholars more than at present; and that parents might rely on their children being carefully instructed. But in spite of the circulars, it is said that, whilst truly zealous in their calling of schoolmasters, the brothers Dalton were neither gainly nor genial in manner, and somewhat deficient in the art of winning the pleasant regards of their pupils. The bucolicism of Eaglesfield still clung to their natures, and manifested itself outwardly in their upright coat-collars, broad-brims, and an unbending fellside Quakerism. As schoolmasters they were severe disciplinarians, exacting silence, order, and a faithful adherence to prescribed rules; the gentlest prating of the little girls, or the smallest blot on a page, called forth rebuke. Admonition was the fact of the hour, and if this did not suffice, the cane or the "tawse," consisting of short leather thongs, was applied to the palm of the hand, and, in worse forms of punishment, to the bare back. Jonathan was looked upon as principal of the school, and was the severer taskmaster. John's more youthful sympathies saved him from so much juvenile reproach; yet my information, derived from their pupils, tends to show that he was far from conciliatory in method, or prone to educe the kindlier parts of his scholars. Their teaching was much more elementary than their curriculum of study indicated. It is said that in the midst of thirty or forty scholars, and all their noisy doings, John found minutes of leisure at his own desk to work out the higher mathematics; if so, he possessed a fifty-schoolmaster-power of abstraction, along with a rare intensity of application.

And so these early years of Dalton's life were spent in Greytown, teaching his Quaker school, and mixing almost wholly with those of his own sect. It was during these twelve years that his frequent visits were made to our valley, all of which took place before his removal to Manchester. There were various inducements for him. In the dale he had fast friends. There were many treasures to be collected, and here his meteorological experiments could be indulged without much fear of ignorant interference. Among the treasures to which I have referred were plants, and Dalton's knowledge of botany would seem to have been considerable. Probably the best testimony to this fact is found in a *Hortus siccus*, comprised in ten volumes, and now in one of the reference libraries at Manchester. Many of these plants were gathered in our valley, and to me the reminiscences conveyed with them are most interesting. I well remember, too, how they had also interested someone else; for, commenting upon the fact that Dalton had written beneath a specimen of the lady's slipper orchid the words, "presented to me by Nancy Wilson," this "someone else" had contributed a note to the effect that over this flower hangs a sweet little veil of romance. "Ah!" he exclaims, "and who was Nancy Wilson? Under what circumstances placed in his (Dalton's) hands? Did it come as an outward and visible sign of something more than 'lute can tell'—something more than a *cypripede?* Eighty years ago, depend upon it, this poor little embrowned blossom was not a blossom only.

But there it is, like the tomb of Cecilia Metella at Rome, and we shall never know any more." I think I could add a little more, but then the tale would be foreign to my subject.

Dalton's life went on much in the same quiet course until his removal to Manchester. He worked hard at school, he lectured, he practised his philosophical experiments, but made few friends. His friendship with the blind Gough, however, was an important, and to him, advantageous one. They had like pursuits, and these often took them afield together. And to nothing did they look forward with such pleasure as a long visit to the dale which I have so frequently mentioned.

CHAPTER X.

I HAVE already told of some of the more notable folk which the valley produced, but as yet I have refrained from giving specimens of the characteristics which caused them to be above the common herd. One of our dalesmen, a yeomen of repute and some standing, was a minute philosopher, and enjoyed the friendship of Mr Wordsworth. Like Gilbert White, he was in the habit of setting down what he saw going on about him; and all his observations are of the most interesting description. He was essentially an outdoor observer; and as he took his facts at first hand from nature, there was always a fascinating freshness about them. One of his more ambitious essays at writing was a sketch, entitled "*The Fisherman: a Character*," a production at once quaint and accurate. After describing the varied charms of the valley, its sweet stream, and the way in which he used to ensnare its crimson-spotted, golden-sided trout, and adding that he must not be tempted to dwell on these reminiscences, he goes on to say, "My present object is an attempt to describe a quaint character whom I met with lately on a morning walk along the road that skirts the aforesaid stream. I had stayed my steps as usual to contemplate, with ever new delight, the features of the valley, when I observed moving down the stream, from just opposite to where I stood, a certain individual who, though not strictly an angler, may be denominated a fisher of the first magnitude. I had not seen him till he moved, but he had seen us, and shifted his position about a hundred yards down the brook, by the side of which he again planted himself. I have known him long, but not intimately; for he is of shy habits, and very chary of all familiar intercourse. I could not but admire his handsome, tall figure as he stood on the bank of the stream, looking into it, 'as if he had been conning a book.' He was arrayed in his constant garb—a durable sort of dress, the colour of dingy white, or rather approaching to a pale blue. The cut or fashion of this costume he never changes, nor does he often renew it—not oftener, I believe, than once a year, when he gets a new suit.

"Your angler is somewhat of an enthusiast, and pursues his gentle craft with an absorbing interest; but then it is only as a pastime and at suitable seasons, when the weather is favourable, when the spring rains have raised the brooks, and dyed their waters with the precious ale colour, and the wind breathes from the mild south; and yet, after all, alas! how often does he return with an empty pannier. It is different with my hero. His sport depends not on the fickle seasons; at least he pursues it in all weathers—in the bright sunshine, or when the face of heaven is overhung with clouds; in the hot days of summer, or when the wind blows from the biting north, and the ponds and streams are bound over with plates of ice; he is still at his work fishing, evermore fishing. Indeed, it must be confessed his very living depends upon it. How often have we pitied him in winter—in a severe winter. It is hard to live upon nothing but fish, and, moreover, to have to catch them before you can dine. It is hard, indeed, to be confined to one dish, and to have no other resource, for if that fail, where are you? It is like the Irishman with his potato—when that rots there is famine. But it has been hinted that my friend is not entirely confined to fish, and that he can occasionally eke out his scanty repast with frogs. I shall not deny it. It is probable enough. It is consoling to have such a resource. In this he but resembles the Frenchman.

"I have said that the angler is an enthusiast, much carried away by his imagination. I have known two or three of this gentle tribe, buoyed up with the hope of sport, set off from our part of the country, walk all the way to Bracken Bridge to try the waters of the silvery Greenwash, and return the same night, after fishing all day, a distance of forty miles, but perhaps not much encumbered by heavy panniers. But if the disciple of Walton is patient and persevering, and takes long rambles in pursuit of his pleasures, I think he is exceeded in every respect by the subject of my description. I believe there is not a tarn or lake, still water with sedgy shore, or running brook with sandy bottom, or even dyke or ditch within a radius of ten miles from his home, that is not well known to him, and in which he has not pursued his solitary sport.

"I have been somewhat puzzled whether to class him as gentleman or poacher, for he partakes of the character of both—a kind of hybrid betwixt the two, neither selling his game, nor, after serving his own needs, disposing of it in any other way, except feeding his children when he happens to have any, and then only while they are of tender age, for they are soon turned out of the parental shelter, and compelled to seek their own living in the world at large, like himself, by fishing. So has it been with his progenitors, so will it be with his posterity till the end of time. As in the East with the Hindoos, and in a degree, with other wanderers like himself, as gipsies and potters, his family seems not to have got beyond the system of caste, which, it must be allowed, shows but a low degree of civilisation. But still, as he sells not his fish, or stoops to any kind of vulgar labour, so far I must rank him as a gentleman. On the other hand, however, as he cannot be called the owner of a single rood of land or water, and yet presumes to sport wherever it suits him, on the property of gentle or simple, yeomen or squire, without condescending to ask leave of any man, I fear, therefore, as far as this goes, I must consider him a poacher. Moreover, like too many of that lawless profession, he is wretchedly poor, and, laying nothing up for a wet day, he must be often, as we hinted before, sorely beset with his wants. There is something in his looks that makes this too probable, the same lank, meagre figure he always was. Let the season be ever so genial, fish ever so plentiful, it makes no difference in his personal appearance; he is as thin and spare as ever, with scarcely an ounce of flesh on his bones. He is emphatically one of Pharaoh's lean kine, seems far gone in consumption, almost like the figure of Death in the old pictures. It was this thin and haggard appearance that led a fanciful French naturalist to describe him as the very type of misery and famine. I suspect, however, that Mons. Buffon was a little out here, and that our hero has more pleasure in life than he was aware of. His patience and persevering efforts must procure him many a savoury meal, and though they do not fatten his ribs, they at least keep him in good working, or rather sporting, order. I trust he will long remain so, and continue to enliven our valley with his presence. Poacher though he be, I respect him for his love of freedom and independence, of nature, and of fishing. We are certain, however fortune may frown upon him, to whatever straits he may be reduced for a living, that rather than seek shelter in a union workhouse he would die of famine.

"I have said nothing of his method of fishing. How various are the arts by which cunning man contrives to circumvent the finny tribe! With all deference to honest Izaak, it must be allowed that the whole art of angling is based upon deceit and imposture. Therefore our sportsman rejects it, we suppose, on that account. And then as to the use of nets, it has doubtless been copied from the villainous spider, who weaves a web from his own bowels, and hangs it before the door of his lair, in which he lurks, ready to pounce upon the unwary victim entangled in its meshes. He will have none of this. Nor does he adopt the more simple and straightforward scheme of the schoolboy and otter, by dragging his speckled prey from under the banks and braes of the populous brooks. No; he has a method of his own. Armed with a single spear-shaped weapon of about six inches in length, woe to the unhappy trout or eel that comes within its range. It is transfixed with the speed of lightning.

"There is no history of an individual from which a moral lesson may not be drawn. Why not, then, from the character of our hero? In a poem of Mr Wordsworth's a fit of despondency is said to have been removed by the patient and cheerful bearing of an old man whom the poet met with on the lonely moors gathering leeches. I have sometimes amused myself in running a parallel betwixt the character I have attempted to describe and the brave old leech-gatherer depicted by Mr Wordsworth. There is no slight resemblance. Both silent and solitary in their habits; both models of patience and perseverance, and of contentment with the calling allotted to them by Heaven; both wanderers; both haunters of ponds and moors, 'from pond to pond he roamed, from moor to moor.' Yes, and on much the same errand, too; for I believe my hero could gather leeches upon occasion (indeed, I durst back him for a trifle were I in the habit of laying wagers) against the old man, both for quickness and tact in that employment. I have, however, no wish that the poet had substituted our hero for his in that noble poem, for I would not alter a line or word of it. I only beg that my fisher may be placed side by side as a teacher of 'resolution and independence' with the immortal leech-gatherer. My sketch has reached a greater length than I had intended, and yet I have only touched on the character of an individual. Perhaps I may be pardoned a few words more on the tribe to which he belongs. Like that of the gipsies and other nomadic races its origin is involved in much obscurity. The probability is that it came from the East, but of its first introduction into Europe I believe history is silent, and the most learned are at a loss on so mysterious a subject. I think, however, it is pretty certain that this wandering tribe had spread widely, and was, perhaps, more numerous than at present, before the barbarians from the North had overrun the Roman Empire.

"Nay, if I might hazard a conjecture, they are so ancient that they date even from beyond the pyramids. Not, however, to indulge in disquisition, but to confine myself strictly to the historic period, I find abundant evidence that they were firmly established in our island during the middle ages, and held in much higher respect than they are at present. Not only were they often present with the baron in his field sports—especially that of hawking—but not seldom in the ancient pastime played a very active part. A still stronger proof of the regard in which they were then held was that, when the lordly baron entertained his numerous followers on grand feast days, the dinner would have been thought very incomplete had they not been present, and then not at the lower end of the long table among the poor retainers, but at the upper part with the most honoured guests. Like the Jews, the people we speak of live in little knots and communities, but not, like them, confined to some dirty quarter of a city, where they can practise the money-making arts. On the contrary our purer race avoids all towns—nay, like the Arab of the desert, they view them with unmingled fear and horror. Never is there one seen there, unless it be some poor captive, pining away his life for want of fresh air and freedom."

. . . . .

Any account of the simple annals of the valley would be incomplete without some description of the hunting in which the people indulged, and I am therefore constrained to give it. One of the great annual hunts took place the day upon which was also held the "Shepherds' Meeting," one of the oldest institutions of the hill districts. This meeting is one which sprung out of the sheep-farming, of necessity. I have before mentioned the fact that there exists at a certain farm in each parish a book setting forth the marks, smits, and ear-slits peculiar to the sheep of each holding in the township. This was in the keeping of some responsible person, and was used as a reference book in case of dispute. It sets forth the name of each farm, the number of its sheep, a rough definition of their range, and the account of each flock is illustrated by cuts. This shows, to take an example, "J. T." on the near shoulder, a red smit down the flank, and the left ear slit down the middle. The slits and smits are essential, for although the initials of the owner may, and frequently do, become blurred and indistinct, the former are lasting, and in case the animals have strayed, they may at once be identified. With the enclosure of the commons, however, this "Smit-Book" is now rarely used, and there is no recent version. If all means of identification failed, the "unkent" sheep were taken on a day to the top of one of the wildest passes in the district to the "Shepherds' Meeting." This was held annually upon the broad summit of High Street, and after the stray sheep were returned to their rightful owners, the day became a festive one. Business done, the shepherds amused themselves with wrestling, racing, leaping, and fox-hunting on foot. And it was at one of the hunts I am about to mention that a man named Dixon fell from an overhanging precipice of about three hundred feet in height, and though terribly bruised and almost scalped, he broke no bones, and recovered from the shock. In falling he struck against the rocks several times, but unconscious the while; immediately on coming to the ground he sprang to his knees, and cried out, "Lads, t' fox is gane out at t' hee end; lig t' dogs on, and I'll cum syun"; then fell down insensible. The place has since borne the name of "Dixon's Three Jumps."

Two packs of hounds are usually present at the meeting—one of harriers, one of fox-hounds. A memorable hunt many years ago was on a glorious day,—the roads ice-bound and the mountains snow-covered. The fields were crusted with hoar-frost, the lakes and tarns with a thin coating of ice, and the fell birds were driven to the valleys. In progressing to the "meet" a beautiful and curious phenomenon was witnessed. On one side Dunmail Raise the sun shone gloriously, whilst on the other a dense mist prevailed. This on its edges was brightened by what resembled a series of rainbows, and the whole effect was one of singular beauty. Upon the side of one of the high-lying valleys the hounds were thrown off, and soon obtained a quest. Puss had been down in the night to feed in the rectory garden, and the hounds told with no uncertain sound how, after quitting the parsley sprays, she had gone through the meadows, out of the fields, across the high road, and into a fir plantation. Being roused from her hiding place among a clump of rushes, she stole quietly out of the wood. But now the voices of the hounds began to rend the thin air with their varied cries, and dashed away, at the same time rousing the echoes of the hills. Knowing well where her strength lay, puss made for the uplands, but being hard pressed, began to retrace her steps. Soon she was back to the plantation which she had so lately left, and three of the leading hounds came topping the fence not far behind. And now, having tried all her devious windings and doubles, "she pants from the place from whence at first she flew." In terror she flies, and is chased by the hounds in full view across the fields, and into an adjoining shrubbery, where she is run into, and killed. Poor puss! one cannot help but exclaim, as her mangled remains are pocketed by a labourer who has been first in at the death. "She'll dae for Sunday dinner, an' I reckon nowt o' jugged hare unless it's been well chowed be t' dogs,"—and so the first hunt ends. After having ale at an inn, generously distributed by the master of the hounds, the whole assembled company again set out and ascend into the region of snow. There is a sprinkling of women and girls, and one or two females belonging to the gentlefolk. From the elevated region, which is soon attained, a glorious prospect presents itself. Lying below is the village of Grasmere, with all its associations. Upon the opposite steeps are Silver Howe and Helm Crag, upon which lie the "lion and the lamb." Easedale and its silent tarn dip between the two heights, and Dunmail between Steel Fell and Seat Sandal. The sun shining upon the snow-clad hills throws up an exquisite rosy flush, and, this being reflected to the valley below, all nature seems bathed in a soft golden light. Here is the ridge of Helvellyn, and we are above the snow line. The hounds have previously been thrown off into a plantation at Fairfield's base, and the huntsman has to use all his skill to prevent the pack from dividing and going off after two diverging hares. And now ensues one of the longest runs of the season. Right along the breast of Fairfield—no shifts or doubles, but straight ahead after the manner of a fox. The hare leads over Fairfield, along the steeps of Nab Scar to Rydal Head, and down into Rydal Vale. The quick ascent over the snow-clad hills from the neighbouring valley has put to the test the stamina of the straggling followers, and three only reach Nab Scar. Here, whilst the hounds are bringing puss back from beneath us, we stop to breathe. Away to the south stretches Windermere with its brown slopes and shaggy copses; Rydal and Grasmere lie below us, whilst over yonder are Esthwaite and Coniston Water; then Easedale, Elterwater, and Blenham Tarns. Far to the south, like a flood of molten fire, stretches Morcambe Bay, with its surrounding hills rolled and lost in cloud. Soon the hounds recross the craggy top, and return in one long line, presenting a pretty picture against the snow. As they take us back along Fairfield many of them are visibly fagged, and the line becomes longer and more straggling. Here a raven, roused, flies off croaking to the nearest glen. The tracks of the hare and hounds are sharply marked against the snow, and something may be read from them. Here puss has run in a circle, and then made a long leap at right angles to her course; but all in vain. The hounds are only baffled for a second, and soon take up the quest. Then the descent begins, and the hare makes back to the woods; and here, to our delight, the dogs are whipped off, everyone agreeing that such a hare is worthy of life, and I only hope that she may never have such a like experience.

Whilst luncheon is getting ready we take a

walk through embosomed Grasmere, which naturally leads us to the side of Wordsworth's grave. There it is, just a plain grassy mound, with its simple inscription of name and date of himself and wife. Near to lie the remains of Hartley Coleridge. The churchyard is green and fresh even now in December. The full Rothay flows just past it, and the yew trees are there as of old. From the churchyard we pass to the church. This contains a bas-relief bust of Wordsworth, with the following inscription:—"To the memory of William Wordsworth, a true philosopher and poet, who, by his special gift and calling of Almighty God, whether he discoursed on man or nature, failed not to lift up the heart to holy things, tired not of maintaining the cause of the poor and simple, and so in perilous times was raised up to become chief minister not only of noblest poesy, but of high and sacred truth. This memorial is placed here by his friends and neighbours, in testimony of respect, affection, and gratitude."

CHAPTER XI.

ALTHOUGH open-air pastimes are, and have always been, few, this does not hold good of those which were enjoyed indoors. From what has been said in recording the annals of our quiet neighbourhood, it will have been gathered that when days were short and nights long, the wits of the young folk must often have been exercised as to how to make the long evenings pass more pleasantly. So far as the inner life of the people has been revealed it will have been seen that the domestic affairs of the dales-folk, especially in the past, were managed with the greatest economy. Although this is very generally true, all suggestion of parsimony vanished when any occasion of festivity came round. Of these occasions Christmas was perhaps the greatest of all. Then the treat in old times circulated from house to house;

and anent this it is striking how little festive occasions have either lapsed or altered. In these early times only the elements of cookery were known, but these elements were often concentrated upon one table in a glorious culmination of dishes. If these would not suggest profusion now, they did then, and prominent among them were several sorts of pies and puddings. Ale "possets" and "fig sue" constituted items of delicacy, and were in great repute among the men and women alike. These things usually formed the chief dishes at supper, although upon great occasions they were given to strangers for breakfast, before the introduction of tea. They were served in bowls, called doublers, into which the company dipped their spoons promiscuously, for the simplicity of the times had not yet seen the necessity of accommodating each guest with a basin or soup plate. The posset-cup held the important place of the champagne cup of to-day. In the better houses it shone as an article of finery. It was made of pewter, and was furnished with two or three lateral pipes, through which the liquid part of the compound might be sucked by those who did not choose the bread. The repast was moistened with malt liquor, which the guests drank out of horns and wooden cans. Cards and conversation constituted the amusements of the elders, whilst the young men entertained the company with exhibitions of maskers, amongst whom the clown was the conspicuous character; and this was varied by parties of rapier dancers, who showed their dexterity in the innocent use of the small-sword. Those more juvenile still conducted themselves noisily in "hunting the rolling pin." This was rather an indelicate amusement (or probably it would be voted so nowadays), and those engaged in it squatted on the floor in a circle, their legs upright, and keeping their hands below their knees. By this arrangement a covered way was formed round the ring, in which the rolling pin moved quickly from hand to hand, being struck frequently against the ground to inform the hunter of its place, who continued running round the circle in pursuit of the flying object.

At the time when these things were in vogue, the country was divided into "latings," from a north country verb "to late" — to seek, to invite. When a death happened, the heads of the houses within the district met to condole with the friends of the deceased, and the younger members watched the corpse through every night until the day of interment. The mistresses of the family met upon the birth of a child, and the occasion was made a festive one. No expense, however, was thrown upon the household most nearly concerned, this being defrayed by the contributions of those present. These two customs are dying out, but even now remain in the more isolated dales. Doles were given to poor persons when a death occurred in a family, and these were not unfrequently sufficient to pay all the funeral charges. Another custom has been referred to in connection with death, which shows the high estimation in which wheaten bread was held by our ancestors. At one time it was considered in the light of a parting gift from the dead to the living. Every person invited to a funeral received a small loaf at the door of the deceased, which it was expected would be carried home. This was a custom of the greatest antiquity, for the people called the loaf *arval* bread—its Latin appellation. The joyousness of a marriage ceremony in old times has been referred to—its being attended by the whole "lating," the cavalcade to church, the race for the riband, and all the rest of the innocent fun. The expense of this, again, was not allowed to fall on the newly-married pair, but was willingly paid by the guests. Then the bride sat in state, and an interesting ceremony commenced. Contributions of money and household utensils were set down before her, which she was asked to accept. So numerous were these gifts, that they frequently constituted almost a start in the new sphere of life upon which the married couple were entering. In connection with these same ceremonies, it ought to be mentioned that it was usual in the dale for guns to be fired over and round the festive house. I have spoken of one of the customs as it used to be, and in a certain vale there exists a remnant of it to-day. Here, for social purposes, the valley is divided into three biddings or latings, corresponding to its three hundreds; and as before these are specially observed in the case of funerals. It is still customary to invite all persons in the "bidding," whether rich or poor; but in the dale dinner is provided at the inn. This repast is certainly not of a funereal character, for roast beef, plum pudding, spiced ale, and other substantial dishes, are provided and freely partaken of.

One of the great festivals of to-day is at sheep-shearing. I have already told how the hill holdings are sheep farms, and that hundreds and sometimes thousands of sheep are grazed on one "heaf." At the washing and shearing of these the dalesmen lend mutual assistance. With almost every dweller in the dale to assist, the "clipping" sometimes lasts a couple of days. After the shearing a feast is given at the farm to which it pertains, and all and sundry are invited to partake of the teeming hospitality; and after this jollity finds its height. There are put in circulation trays of tobacco, ale, spirits, and a series of most inspiriting ballads. Those who do not care for this kind of entertainment in the spacious barn, make to the fell side, and there indulge in athletic sports—wrestling, foot racing, and leaping, the best wrestler being rewarded with the finest fleece of the clip. An Auld Wives' Hake is another festivity once common in the fell districts, and usually held on Christmas Eve. At one time it was observed by matrons only; and the evening was spent in drinking tea, "telling stories of dark complexion," and much gossip and scandal was indulged in. Where such festivities are held nowadays the young folk have broken in, and the character of the entertainment is modified. In these dancing and singing would seem to form the principal items. The herb-puddings which it is customary to eat at Easter may be reminiscences of Easter tansies. All the villagers attend the hill churches on Easter Sunday, and take with them garlands of such wild flowers as are "out." "Nut Monday

SHEEP SHEARING IN THE DALES.

is another holiday — a recreation in which most young people delight, being a merry harvesting play, that leads away to the bosky hill slopes, where on either side, between the overhanging rocks, the hazels grow heavily laden, bending to the stream. It leads away to the woods where meeting hazels darken under stately trees whose dense foliage is all aglow with the most gorgeous tints that nature's matchless pencil can impart; where the squirrel, prettiest of wood-land creatures, elfin lord of the hazel bushes, resents the intrusion upon his domains, and from the summit of his watch tower — a tall oak — looks down on the intruders with scintillating eyes, and perks his ears, and stamps, and cries aloud. All true lovers of nature, indeed, squirrels, dormice, monkeys, and men, like nutting. Wordsworth, nature's high priest, tells us that the day on which, when a schoolboy at Hawkshead, he sallied forth,

> "Tricked out in proud disguise of cast-off tweeds,
> With a huge wallet o'er his shoulders slung,

A-nutting, crook in hand,
Was like many another day he thus employed—
One of those heavenly days that cannot die.

"They have always fine weather when they go a-nutting—poets and people of that ilk. Look at plump and pleasant Miss Mitford, what a lucky lassie was she? For the day on which she sallied forth might have been made for the purpose, being one of those delicious autumnal days when the air, the sky, and the earth seem lulled into a delicious calm. Well might she exclaim, 'Oh, what an enjoyment nutting is.' Who wouldn't have liked to have been with her when, as she tells us, she doffed her shawl, tucked up her flounces, twisted her straw bonnet into a basket, and gathered and scrambled the thick-clustering brown leemers, while her favoured companion hooked down the bushes. It is a wonder he didn't hook her; for she was fat and fair, and if half so rich as her writings and her nut-basket what a prize she must have proved! But, content with her name and her fame, her village, her flower garden and filbert groves, she chose the better part, and, considering with the Apostle that though it might be good to marry it was better not, remained in single blessedness through all the happy Nut Mondays of her life."

Only those who have themselves lived in an isolated dale can form any idea of its loneliness. This, however, refers more to the dark days of winter, than to the brighter ones of summer. Whatever the time, the sheep claim the attention of the farm workers. Yesterday I went to the Hall, where I saw the cream from twenty-three cows being converted into yellow, fragrant butter. But such a number of milchers is altogether unusual. The Hall farm happens to lie at the head of the dale, and much land about it has been reclaimed from the wide-spreading beck. The river-bed has cut deeper, and by liming and draining the side strips, a number of meadows have been won to the farm. This work was done a few years ago, and with liberal treatment the fields have yielded fodder abundantly. But this state of things is quite exceptional, and usually only a few milch cows are kept. As I have frequently repeated, the hill holdings are sheep farms. The yeomen talk of sheep, and everywhere about the farms various objects testify to their presence. The heaf-going sheep at the Hall farm number 1500 to 2000, a somewhat larger number than belongs to the ordinary steadings. The breed of sheep which find food upon the mountains are either herdwicks or small black-faced, which are said to be peculiar to the district. The story of the introduction of a kind of sheep which so well suits its environment is a somewhat curious one. It has reference to the herdwick. It is said that a great many years ago a strange ship stranded upon the Cumberland coast, and the only living things upon it were a flock of sheep, of a kind which before had not been seen. These either swam or were brought ashore, and some of the yeomen of Wastdale Head drove them up the sides of the fells. When winter and the snowstorms came, these sheep, instead of making to the sheltered spots, immediately sought out the exposed peaks of the bleak fell tops, where, the wind driving hard, the snow was unable to lodge. As the sheep had always this resource, they were but rarely buried in the drifts, and proved themselves peculiarly appropriate to the mountains. The herdwicks are probably much older in the hill districts than this legendary story which introduces them. One of the valuable characteristics of the breed is that it has what the farmer calls a "jacket and waistcoat"—a layer of soft thick wool close to the body beneath the longer staple of the fleece. This, then, is the variety of sheep which is found in the valley and is peculiar to the hill ranges around. By selection, the special characteristics which fit it for its elevated home are reproduced again and again, until now they have become fixed. At one time—before the enclosure of the commons—it was necessary that the sheep belonging to a certain farm should be localised upon their own allotment; but now that the commons are enclosed this is no longer necessary. This was insured by a tenant, on giving up his farm, leaving (say) a fifth of his sheep of the old "heaf," these being purchased by his successor at a fair valuation. If the whole flock was allowed to remain on like conditions, so much the better for the incoming tenant.

It is the tending of the sheep then that is so closely associated with the life of the statesman. About his farm are quaint stone folds in which the sheep are penned when they are brought home on any particular occasion during the year. Even in winter they can scrape a precarious existence from the bare fells, but when it is practicable they are moved to lower levels at the coming of the first snow. When this cannot be accomplished, hay is taken by the shepherds upon their backs, and the sheep are foddered on the fells. If this is imperative the winter life of the shepherd is a hard one, both for himself and dogs, and the farmers often suffer considerable loss. With the exercise of all their instinct, the sheep—both herdwick and black-faced—not unfrequently become buried in the drifts, and have to be dug out. Under these circumstances they can live for a considerable time, and have been known to be rescued alive after a fortnight's entombment. At the digging out of a number of sheep at which I was present, the poor creatures were in a terribly weak and exhausted condition, and had eaten the wool off each other's backs. It is marvellous, however, how these goat-like creatures survive winter and come out of it in even fair condition. It is when winter is unusually severe, and the snow lies long on the hills, that the greatest casualties occur. In one case, two years ago, 1500 sheep died on the hills out of a flock of 6000. But in time spring sends its genial influences abroad, and the snows begin to melt. The mist caps rise from the peaks, and the foam of the fell becks sparkles as it leaps among the rocks. As the snow recedes before the warm sun, the turf comes green beneath it and daily gains in growth. If the sheep be observed, it will be seen that their heads are all turned towards the skyline, and they seem to nibble as though for very life. The voice of the shepherd and his dogs is now heard daily upon the fells, and there is a joyousness in the warm air. The boulder-strewn slopes are at this time enlivened by the return of the mountain birds, and the first spring flowers begin to respond to the sun. As April passes into May the sheep have much improved in condition, and by the end of the month, if the weather be seasonably warm, the washing of the flocks is taken in hand. The critical lambing time has passed by June, and the lambs and their dams are together enjoying the sweet green grass of the slopes. On the day prior to that on which the washing is intended to take place, the shepherd goes to the hills with his full complement of canine helpers. Every nook and cranny of the ghylls and crags is sought by the nimble collies, and not a sheep is left behind—or rarely so. Although the slopes may only show scattered sheep here and there, it is seen how the numbers gain and the flock grows as it becomes concentrated. When the gathering is completed, the sheep are driven slowly down dale, travelling so as not to tire the lambs, and that they may pick their way unhurt over the sharp stones. The very foot of the valley has to be sought, as here the large deep dubs of water are found in which the grey fleeces are to be whitened. The sheep washing is quite a primitive and a pleasant festival. Rude folds are constructed by the stream side, and a "washer" wades into a deep pool. One by one the sheep are thrown in by a couple of stalwart dalesmen, and each sheep in turn is thoroughly soused and rinsed. When all the foreign matter has been abstracted from the fleece the dripping animal is allowed to swim ashore. This is slow and heavy work, and often two or three long summer days are taken to accomplish it. The sheep dry quickly, and afford a pretty sight as their whitened fleeces pick out the tender green of the grass. There is a great bleating between the lambs and their dams, but this gradually dies away. If the sheep have been washed upon their own ground, they are not driven back to the higher runs, but are allowed to climb out to the fell-tops themselves. This they soon accomplish, and next morning the sheep walks present their usual appearance. A month goes by and the warmth increases. The wool becomes an encumbrance, and a long summer night of "gathering" again takes place. There are only about a couple of hours of darkness, when the collecting must cease; and now the shepherds wrap themselves in their plaids, and munch some refreshment under the side of a boulder. With the first faint streaks of light both men and dogs are again busy, and once more the flocks converge upon the mountain road. When the men and their flocks arrive at the farm they find all their neighbours arrived to help with the shearing, and soon the metallic click of the shears is heard far down dale. I have, however, already described the "clipping," and now we must come to its close, when the sheep are once more driven to the fells. It is then that is seen one of the prettiest sights which the day affords. Turned into the long lanes, the white fleeceless flock presents an indescribable picture of pastoral beauty. Every sheep hangs upon the hazel-clad slopes, stretching its quiet neck to the tender herbage. Not a foot of the bank seems unoccupied—two long lines of sleek, browsing sheep reaching away until a bend in the road hides them. The babel of sound which was heard a few minutes ago becomes less general, then it ceases, and a strange stillness fills the lane. We do not see the flock again until autumn, when a new fleece has grown, and the sheep are brought down to be "dipped."

CHAPTER XII.

OF the many changes between "then" and "now," there is one even in the dales which is most marked. The horse which the hill farmer brings to market has changed, so have his cattle, and not least so himself. But his womenkind, his daughters, have changed more than all. And I will here set down what I have observed in this relation, though having more general application than to the narrow boundaries of our valley. Domesticity among English girls is probably at a lower ebb now than it has been for a couple of centuries. Many of the home arts, which once formed an important part of domestic daily life, are fast decaying, or have died out. This is perhaps less so in the country than in towns, but even in the former female manners have much changed of late. There is little of that simplicity which was so characteristic of the past century girl, which made her life a reflex of a pure yet healthy animalism. She was essentially "homely," had homely ways and used homely phrases. Her pleasures were mostly indoors, and her pastimes of a profitable nature. There was scarcely an article of wear of which she was not architect and constructor; and it just as frequently happened that the original material was partly manufactured by her own hands. Then spinning wheels were in every country house, and every yeoman and farmer was a small manufacturer. One of the great indoor employments of winter evenings was this spinning within the ingle nook. Of course, the wool had to be first combed, and it was then piled in snowy heaps to feed the ravenous spindles. At the times of which I write, fields of flax were part of every northern demesne, the hemp being spun and made into skirts and shirts. Yarn hose and coarse druggets were also articles of common manufacture, but these have long gone out. In short, spinning of whatever kind is lost as a domestic art, the whole female population having turned its back on honest homespun. Nearly every past century country house of the north contained quaint oaken arks and chests, the contents of which invariably testified to the ability and worth of the women. They were stored with quantities of linen and woollen cloths, all the produce of home industry.

In nearly all cases a portion of this formed the bride's only dowry, and lucky was the young yeoman who secured a wife with "a chest of fine linen cloth." The mistress of a great house possessed a thorough knowledge of all the domestic arts, as well as the designing and working of artistic tapestry. Every female from nine to ninety—and longevity was one of the great characteristics of the fell folk—was a wondrous knitter, and the northern "out-

put" of blue-grey stockings was enormous. These were carried by pack-horses to the large southern towns, and formed a staple article of industry.

The Arkwrights of the period produced the innumerable rudely-carved arks and chests which are so characteristic of northern houses. In these the home manufactures were deposited, and they contained many things besides. They were intended for the preservation of conserves, oaten cake, and dried meats. These latter were an important part of the food supply which, taken throughout the year, was altogether inadequate to the demands of the community. The feeding and fattening of cattle was but little understood, for the stock fed in autumn being killed off by Christmas, very little fresh meat appeared in the markets before the ensuing midsummer. The yeomen and manufacturers provided against this inconvenience by curing a quantity of beef in autumn, part of which was pickled in brine, the rest being dried in the smoke of the capacious chimneys. The pickling was performed by the women, and successful preserving was one ot the great arts of the time. Cooking, however, was at a low ebb ; each family boiled sufficient salt provision on Sunday to last for the week, and this and oatmeal pudding constituted the chief meal of the day. The women were great adepts at making oaten cake, which was made in large circular layers. Two or three days were specially set aside for this work, and sufficient was made to last the family for twelve or thirteen weeks. All these things were stored in the before-mentioned arks. The female portion of the household attended to the poultry, geese, and calves, these, with the addition of eggs, constituting the whole of the fresh food for winter. Poached salmon was sometimes added, but as this was out of season it was insipid and watery. The veal was ill-fed and ill-favoured, the calves being carried to market when only two or three weeks old. About this time tea found its way to the north from the metropolis, being brought by the woollen merchants. In spite of opposition by the men, it soon became the favourite beverage. Its qualities and preparation were at first but little understood. One old lady—and she a dame of standing—received a quantity from her son in London, which she smoked instead of tobacco. Another housewife converted a present of a like nature into a herb-pudding of considerable dimensions, which, not proving palatable, she dressed with such spices as she possessed, but failed to subdue its bitterness. Porcelain followed the introduction of tea,

displacing the neatly turned cups and saucers of maple; and wheaten flour was rarely seen except in the houses of the rich.

The yeoman had few of the objects of elegance and ease which the same class—where it exists—has to-day. They were a practical people, but their practice has not come down to their descendants. Our women and girls have rushed to the other extreme. The ordinary arts of knitting and sewing are being year by year lost to general womanhood. Their qualifications for the offices of wife and mother are few, and it is deplorable to have to believe that they are becoming fewer.

One of the great institutions of the valley was the country carrier. With his slowly rolling cart and old horse, he was an all important individual, and performed a multitudinous number of offices. It was perhaps because he could neither read nor write that he had such a marvellous memory, and this was essential to his compound trade. He made journeys twice a week to Greytown, and upon these occasions carried commissions from nearly every one in the dale. These ranged from strings of beads to sacks of flour, and from pins to new gowns. There was nothing which might be required that the carrier could not bring, and with his many-sided character he had a marvellous power of pleasing everybody. In many cases the carrier brought the whole of the groceries for the year, and a hundred things besides. It mattered not of how great a number of items his individual orders consisted; he always rendered a faithful and accurate account upon his return. And even his enemies had to admit that he could do this even when often otherwise than sober. These would relate how sometimes they had seen the carrier's legs only visible over the front of the cart, his upper three-fourths at the time being sonorously dreaming among sacks of flour, beer barrels, and a hundred other miscellaneous articles. But then, as I have said, these were his enemies, and, if there was truth in the statement, it was somewhat strange that no mishap ever occurred, and that after these rumours the carrier always appeared with his honest, serious face, looking very innocent through all its russet bluffness. Dobbin, the carrier's horse, was almost as wonderful a compound as the carrier himself, and the enemies already referred to even asserted that Dobbin was endowed with a higher intelligence than its master. Of course, this was a gross libel, though they asserted, by way of confirmation, that upon occasions when "Willum" had slipped down between the horse and cart, the sagacious creature had stood stock still until some passer-by had dragged him out and replaced him upon the front of the cart. However this may be, I know "Willum" himself had infinite faith in the old horse, and he has told me how on dark winter evenings, when the snow lay thickly in the dale roads, he has given Dobbin his head and let him plough through the deep drifts home, and how he always succeeded in doing this without mishap. When by himself, Dobbin could open all the gates with wooden latches and let himself through, and in this capacity he sometimes brought "Willum" into wordy collision with his neighbours on account of his lax notions of *meum* and *tuum*. The old horse had a fatality for opening gates of fields which contained pasturage better than his own, and seemed quite unconcerned whether the same was intended for haygrass or no. But the time when the carrier and his cart were most characteristic was when they were met on the road. The latter was covered in with a huge canvas dome that served to keep off both rain and sun. The heavy rolling cart was invariably enveloped in a cloud of dust in summer, and a cloud of moisture in winter. There were two accompaniments to the cart which were never absent. One of these was an old-world horn lantern which swung beneath it, the other a large dog which kept faithful watch and ward when "Willum" was asleep or overcome by drowsiness. But the old carrier has turned off the road to another bourne, and such are the innovations of the time that there is none to succeed him.

The dalesmen go to market much more frequently than of yore, and it would sometimes appear that they go because it is market day and by no means of necessity. Time was when attending Greytown was quite an event—at least to the younger members of the family; now it is unusual if they stay at home. These facts will suggest that the houses of the yeomen are changed in their economy, which is true; and the change is probably for the better. They have many creature comforts, which cost but little, and to which they were once strangers. They are brought somewhat nearer to the world of life, too, and know something of what goes on there. And, best of all, they have been made acquainted with books, which more than all tend to enliven and refresh their lonely lives.

There is one other "institution" which was connected with the dale, though he could hardly be said to be of it. This was the postman. He did not actually come into the dale, but brought the letters to the foot of the valley, and left them either in a hollow tree or at the smithy. In proceeding from Greytown, however, he blew a horn at the lane ends to call the country folk if there happened to be any communication for them. By this arrangement the postman was saved the trudging of many a weary mile, and was enabled to keep pretty much to the beaten highway. He could sound a blast on his horn which would be heard nearly over the parish, and the signal proved a most effective one. And then he was rarely kept waiting. A letter was an important arrival, which often constituted an era in itself, and the postman's horn occasionally sent consternation through a family; and well it might, for a letter was a letter in those days. Such epistles were not penned lightly. Writing a letter was not a thing to be taken hastily in hand. The task was often talked about for many days ere its accomplishment, and its contents were the outcome of many heads. And this will be better understood when the subject of such letter writing is known. Nothing but a birth, a marriage, or a death could induce a sturdy yeoman to reduce the facts of the same to paper; or to convey some rough, honest sympathy to those who had to bear the brunt of affliction. Even such occasions as these, when the people were poor, were not always productive of a letter, and the friends outside their little world were not made cognisant of sad or joyous facts until long months after, when perhaps some accident revealed it. Under these circumstances it will not be difficult to understand that the better-class yeoman sometimes received a letter each week, whilst others could only boast that number in a year. This office of postman, with all its importance, is deeply impressed on my memory from the fact that I once filled it. During the summer vacation, when the loneliness of the dale became even painful to me as a very small boy, I was not unfrequently thrown on the back of an old cart mare, and, with only a halter for trappings, was sent from the head to the foot of the dale once a week to see after letters. If two or three were to be found at the smithy, or, higher, in an old oak, I rejoiced exceedingly, and turned the head of the mare homewards very much conscious of the fact that I constituted at the time "Her Majesty's Mail." In many cases the letters received were ranged upon the chimney-piece to show, in some measure, the importance of the family.

Two other characters who frequented the valley, but were not of it, were a pedlar and an old fern gatherer. The first was a type of a class of men once common but now nearly extinct. They carried packs on their backs, and spent months in tramping the country, and in going from farm to farm to show their wares. The pack contained a very miscellaneous assortment of small things likely to excite the interest of the women and girls especially, and the pedlar was always a welcome guest. He was newsman, too, and told to the credulous dalesfolk all that was happening in the outside world, and a great deal that was not. He stayed at the farm where night happened to find him, though there was sometimes competition for his company. Of course he was garrulous, but at the same time he was fairly honest; and it was from a compound of this class of men that Wordsworth drew the life and character of his immortal "Wanderer."

In spring and summer the boulder-strewn slopes of the valley were everywhere covered with beautiful and rare ferns; and the old fern-gatherer came to collect them. He was as

BN 1894

constant in his coming as the pale green fronds of the ferns themselves, and his presence was always welcome. He used to carry hampers full of ferns to his home in Greytown, and there he put them into pretty rustic baskets made from the lesser hazel boughs. In autumn he gathered nuts and cresses, all of which he turned into money. The old man was a fairly good naturalist, and the pursuit he had chosen we always believed came from a strong love of nature.

CHAPTER XIII.

IT was rarely that anything occurred in the valley to arouse the dwellers out of the even tenor of their way; and looking back over a long life not more than two or three such incidents suggest themselves. I have already stated that the vale was but rarely invaded, and at long intervals. Among these invaders were rambling botanists, and sometimes a geologist armed with his hammer. These visitors were generally looked upon by the dalesfolk as harmless individuals, though as lacking something mentally. The great Prof. Sedgwick often visited the dale in summer, and upon one occasion a gentleman presented the genial Professor with a shilling, being, as the stranger expressed it, such an "exceedingly intelligent old man."

Everywhere dotted among the hills are small mountain tarns, each a veritable paradise to the wandering botanist and angler. In the neighbourhood of the valley one can rarely walk far without coming across them in the hollows of the mountains; and as I have had occasion to mention them so often, and they form such a characteristic feature, I may be excused if I set down somewhat minutely a description of one of them—one which I almost look upon as my own possession.

At the base of Breeda is a shimmering lakelet, nestling at the foot of the great green hills. And around the mere is my mountain garden. To the hundred wild denizens the tarn must prove a veritable summer paradise; and those hills beyond are surely the Delectable Mountains. The marsh-plants and bog-birds have chosen well their haunt, and even now revel in the wealth of summer. The tarn is done in a setting of pale green reeds, these again by waving rushes. The cool leaves of the waterlilies float on every tiny wavelet. Myriads of delicate bank-swallows cling to the giant rushes, whose slender stems bow beneath their weight; then one just touches the water and leaves a sweet commotion in ever widening circles long after it has flown.

In those dark-green depths a shoal of silvery roach is falling and rising in the warm sunlight, and here a pike rushes off through the reeds. The waterhen leads out her brood among the lilies, and black coots call from the lush summer grass. A pair of swans, whose whole existence seems spent above their shadow, have built a rude structure of a nest, and soon the brown cygnets will take possession of the tarn. The green glint of the "water-wolf" shows as it makes for the deeps. A pair of sandpipers, or summer-snipe, run over the pebbles and drift-stuff, and then with tremulous wings make across the mere. That restless, delicate reed-warbler has its nest and its game-preserves among the rushes, and ceaselessly runs up and down the stalks of the bog-plants. Its beautifully domed nest is interwoven with and supported by four reed stems, and sways gently in the wind. Sometimes it even touches the water but the brown eggs are safe in their soft setting. Another bird of this wild weed garden is the garrulous little sedge-warbler—a veritable mocking-bird, that seems to spend its existence in imitating the birds of the marsh.

But the bog-plants—the exquisite floral denizens of the tarn. There, deep down in the flags, are the sinuous roots of the water-buttercup. Its star-like flowers float on the water—delicate white crowns set in gold. The yellow and purple irises tower over all, their great sword-like leaves the haunt of myriad dragon-flies. These are everywhere sailing above the warm water in vesture of blue and gold. Pretty spiral shells, just half immersed, are dotted over the mere, and constitute the freshwater nautilis of their mountain home. Set everywhere along the marge are tufts of woodruff, which emit an aroma as of newly-mown hay. The tiny white flowers are tinged with pink, and are "sweetest when crushed." Growing in close communion is the rose-coloured marsh - orchis and pink valerian. Where an old wall runs down to the tarn there is a great golden patch of globe-flower—a rare and cultivated plant in many districts, but here growing wild. Even now a group of laughing school girls are returning from the mere garlanded with the golden flowers. A bunch of blue vetchling lights up the bog, and this mare's-tail takes us back to an old-world fossil flora. The blue marsh vetchling is rare in its beauty, and blooms side by side with the Grass of Parnassus. Shadowing the sundew and pimpernel is the elegant bog-asphodel with its star-like flower. These were formerly used by ladies for dyeing the hair yellow. Its companion, the curiously fringed sundew, is one of the few British insectivorous plants—a vegetable fly-trap. Not only are the insects held fast by a viscid substance which covers the leaves, but its sensitive hairs quickly close upon any unfortunate victim, and do not relax their hold until death ensues. Everywhere over the bog, cotton-grass waves its snowy plumes, and a dozen species of sedges toss their bearded heads to the breeze. Resting on our oars, a blue heron flaps slowly over the mere, and takes its sentinel stand on the further side.

The loveliest marsh plant, however, of my mountain garden is the frosted buck-bean. Its cluster of blossoms, before fully expanded, are rose coloured, and when open the petals are covered with a silken, plush-like fringe. It is the "flower of liberty" of the Danes, though their idea that it is found only within their own country is quite an erroneous one.

There, half in the water, are the brilliant blue petals of the germander speedwell, and close by its little cousin, veronica montana. Glistening among the reeds are the brilliant corollas of the blue brook-lime, or water-purpie, as the Scotch love to call it. Pushing our old slimy punt in among the rushes, we disturb a pair of reed-sparrows which have their nest deep down in the flags; and a few yards further on a pair of wild ducks get up heavily from the tarn, and make off with outstretched necks. Stepping out a yard from the punt is a great bunch of dusky cranesbill, and lesser tufts of eye-bright—a plant with high virtues according to the herbalists. Beautiful to our eyes is the little scarlet pimpernel,—poor man's weather-glass, or shepherd's barometer. All these names are appropriate, for not only do its flowers close at the approach of rain, but open and close both morning and afternoon with the greatest regularity. The pimpernel is one of the only two scarlet British wild flowers, and is extremely beautiful. It is a low creeping plant, and here runs out from the edge of the marsh into the cornfields as though to cultivate the acquaintance of the scarlet poppy. Returning to the tarn, all the water plantains are here; the family of the duck-weeds, and, upon a mass of tangle, is the floating nest of a coot. The curious aloe-like water-soldier is here; and were not anacharis the principal food of the swans and their cygnets it would soon fill the tarn.

So many rare or beautiful plants grow in

my mountain garden as to be almost innumerable. Just where a tiny stream joins the mere the evening primrose grows in great luxuriance. Its old name of winetrap it has from the fact of its being, at one time, used as an incentive to winedrinking, as olives are to-day. Brightening up the edges of the bog are great golden tufts of marsh-marigold, which has bloomed since spring, and will continue right on to the end of summer. The lilac valerian is here, the horse-tail, and the bugloss. Floating in the shallower parts of the tarn are the large white clustering blossoms of the frogbit. The crumpled petals are just tinged with pink, their satiny surface looking like mother-of-pearl in its iridescent hues. As a setting for the flowers are the cool, glossy leaves on their long floating stalks; and it is perhaps on this account that the older botanists called the plant lesser water-lily. The delicate rose-coloured flowers of the pretty bog pimpernel peep from the marsh turf, and the likeness of its flowers to tiny fragile rock roses is quite striking. This and many of the plants of my mountain garden are among the gems of our valley flora; but most curious among them all is a tiny floating water-weed—the bladder-wort. This is a subtle fish-poacher, the true character of which has only lately been detected. Along its branches are a number of small green vesicles or bladders, which, being furnished with tiny jaws, seize upon the little fish, which are quickly assimilated into its substance.

Sandwort, bog-rush, and stitchwort elbow each other for existence, and everywhere the flutter of wings shows that birds love the tarn as well as plants. The quaint water-avens look like hooded nuns in their curious brown petals, and show as one of the prettiest and most prominent flowers of the tarn. Last of all is the Grass of Parnassus, with its handsome cream-coloured flowers marked with darker veins. With nothing grass-like about it, it rears its graceful head to the soft summer breeze, and is perhaps the most beautiful of all the floral denizens of my mountain garden.

* * * * *

The making of provision of *fire-elden* for the winter was perhaps one of the dalesfolks' most important occupations. Peat constituted the general fuel, for coal was inaccessible. Nature was lavish in her provision, and the moors above the valley abounded in it. The beds were in immense thickness, and this and the purity of the brown *humus* attested the presence of primitive forests. Many of the hill ranges are still forests in name, but vestiges of timber are but sporadic and sparse. Peat is, of course, of forest growth. Twigs and branches of birch, oak, and alder are plain among the layers; and it is so good a mummifier that you can even trace the venation of the leaves, while the great trunks of blackened oak dug from the bogs are still so sound that the yeomen use them for beams and other offices where strength and durability are essential. Acorns, too, and beech-mast and hazel-nuts are all found in comparative freshness; and therewith remains of races that have passed away—the bones of wolves, of red deer, fallow, and roe, and vanished species of birds, the tusks of wild boars, and sometimes a stone implement—a relic of primitive man. The peat grows abundant crops of heather for the grouse; while the plateaux are grazing for young cattle in summer and for sheep throughout the year. Here, too, the hill-fox feeds her young, and fattens them on grouse and plover; and here the naturalist finds his happiest hunting grounds.

Just as every sheep-farmer has right of "heaf" upon the fell, so has he right of "turbary" on the moor; and this quite irrespective of ownership or tenancy of turfy parts. Cutting—or "graving"—the peat is done in early summer. It is hard work, but the farm hands like the change. They go out in the morning and come back late at night. The grass and the bents are first stripped from the turf in layers of considerable thickness, which are used for roofing outhouses, cartsheds, and sheepfolds. The spade called a "slane," has one-half of the cutting part bent at right angles to the other, and the peat is cut inversely to its line of deposit or cleavage—a method that admirably reveals the manner in which it has been deposited. The richest is squared into rectangular blocks, eight by four inches, and two inches thick. A stalwart Westmerian can "grave" a considerable quantity in a day; but graving is not all. The rough blocks have to be shaped and stacked to insure a thorough drying. The stacks are so built that the air circulates freely about and through them, and at a distance they look like so many huge dolls' houses. As summer passes, the shepherds look at them as they happen to be their way; and when they are dry, then "leading" begins. The peat cannot be brought from the moor in carts, but is led in rude and primitive sledges. There is nothing to prevent these from over-running the galloways harnessed to them, but accidents are rare. The moorland slopes that lead from the "lots" are exceedingly precipitous, and sledding, as the men call it, is rough work. When the peat has all been brought down it is again stacked, this time in outhouses. A "stick-heap" is an invariable accessory in the fold, with a huge

log whereon to chop the coppice-wood poles into lengths for the fire; and the ring of the axe from the farmyards is a characteristic and cheerful winter sound.

www.ingramcontent.com/pod-product-compliance
Lightning Source LLC
LaVergne TN
LVHW091132080826
845145LV00008B/2130

* 9 7 8 1 4 7 3 3 3 7 8 9 3 *